D0040692

INVASION OF THE SCORP-LIONS

A Monstertown Mystery

INVASION OF THE SCORP-LIONS!

A Monstertown Mystery

by Bruce Hale

DISNEP • HYPERION

Los Angeles   New York

First Edition, October 2017
1 3 5 7 9 10 8 6 4 2
FAC-029191-17258
Printed in Malaysia

This book is set in ITC Garamond Std/Monotype;
Abagail, P22 Garamouche/Fontspring
Designed by Rachna Batra

Library of Congress Cataloging-in-Publication Data
Names: Hale, Bruce, author.
Title: Invasion of the scorp-lions : a Monstertown mystery / by Bruce Hale.
Other titles: Invasion of the scorpions
Description: First edition. Los Angeles ; New York : Disney-Hyperion,
2017. Summary: When a classmate falls into a coma, best friends and
monster hunters Carlos and Benny investigate weird noises and smells
that are coming through Monterrosa Elementary's classroom vents.
Identifiers: LCCN 2016020840 • ISBN 9781484713235 (reinforced binding)
Subjects: CYAC: Monsters—Fiction. Schools—Fiction.
Best friends—Fiction. Friendship—Fiction. Genetic
engineering—Fiction. Mystery and detective stories.
Classification: LCC PZ7.H1295 Inv 2017 • DDC [Fic]—dc23
LC record available at https://lccn.loc.gov/2016020840

Reinforced binding
Visit www.DisneyBooks.com

To Stephanie, ace editor and partner in crime,
with mucho aloha

THE ONLY THING more dangerous than a dare is a double-dog dare. Most kids I know are powerless to resist one, and Benny Brackman and I were no exceptions. That's why nighttime found us creeping around the school's mechanical room searching for a ghost—despite common sense, good judgment, and the risk of missing my favorite TV show.

"Darn Tyler Spork," said Benny. He shone his black-light flashlight into a shadowy corner behind one of the massive boilers.

"We didn't *have* to take his dare," I said.

Benny gave me The Look. It could mean different things

at different times, but just then it meant *Stop being a total doofus, Carlos.*

"No, really," I said, playing my own flashlight beam over cobwebs big enough to snare a Buick. "What kind of fool deliberately risks supernatural danger, just on a dare?"

Benny smirked. "Have you looked in the mirror lately?"

He was right, so I ignored him.

I turned slowly, taking in the room. It was chilly and grim, smelling of dust, oil, and that funky wet-cat-with-gas odor we'd come to associate with whatever was haunting our school. The room was packed with pipes and ducts and mysterious machines. Darkness enfolded it, except for our lights and a faint red glow from the control boards.

The perfect place for a paranormal ambush.

The tiny hairs on my neck raised as my imagination kicked into gear. I pictured headless skeletons, leering monsters, creatures made of ectoplasm and raw, bloody flesh. (Yes, I watch too many movies.)

Something skittered behind a boiler.

"What was that?" I whipped around, aiming my flashlight toward the noise.

In the purplish-black light, Benny's eyes glowed as huge and white as brand-new volleyballs. "I d-dunno," he whispered. "Do ghosts make that kind of noise?"

"You've known me since kindergarten. Have I ever mentioned meeting a ghost?"

Slowly, ever so carefully, we crept past thick conduit pipes that would've looked right at home in Dr. Frankenstein's laboratory. At the far edge of the boiler, Benny and I paused, gathering our courage.

He nodded, and together we peeked around the corner.

I gasped.

"Whoa!" cried Benny.

The creature captured in our flashlight beams was no ghost. No animated skeleton. In fact, it was so strange I couldn't wrap my mind around it.

The thing looked . . . wrong, somehow.

Roughly the size of a pit bull, it glowered up at us with the hungry amber stare of a big cat. Its head and muscular body resembled a lion, but two thick pincers, like those of a crab, curved forward from its chest, clicking and snapping. Segmented armor plates along the spine led to a thick scorpion tail, which arched forward, dripping poison.

Not exactly the kind of thing you want to meet in a dark room. Or even a well-lit one. My heart thudded so irregularly, it felt like it was beat-boxing.

The creature hissed, tail twitching.

Benny and I stumbled back.

"What the heck?" he rasped.

I backed into a pipe with a *thunk*. Behind us, another hiss.

"I'm not sure," I said, shining my light toward the sound, "but I think it's got a friend."

My beam found a second monster, right behind me. It

3

snarled, bared some serious fangs, and bowed its chest to the ground like a playful puppy. But this thing was no puppy.

"*¡Híjole!*" I swayed, off-balance.

"Look out, Carlos!" cried Benny.

The creature's tail lashed forward at me. My feet seemed frozen in place, as its razor-sharp stinger plunged down, down . . .

Ugh, I've done it again. I started my story at an exciting spot, like our teacher always says to, but I forgot to mention a few important things. Like who Benny and I are. Like what's going on. And like how we ended up in a room full of monsters in the first place.

I don't know how authors do it; this writing stuff is *hard*.

Maybe I should take you back to the beginning. No, not to the day I was born. The day we realized that someone, or some*thing*, was terrorizing Monterrosa Elementary, and that someone (namely Benny and I) had to do something about it.

Chapter One

Coma Chameleon

THE FIRST THING you need to know about my teacher Mr. Chu is that although he used to be a were-hyena (a whole 'nother story), he's one of the best teachers at Montorrosa Elementary. The second thing to know is, when he teaches a subject, he *really gets into it.*

So I guess I shouldn't have been surprised when Benny and I returned from lunch to find that our entire classroom had transformed into an ancient Greek temple, with fake pillars and all. Mr. Chu stood at the front of the room wrapped in a white bedsheet, a wreath of green leaves perched on his bald head.

"Welcome, citizens!" he bellowed, strumming some kind of horseshoe-shaped harp.

"Citizens of Crazyville," muttered Tyler Spork, taking his seat. But I could tell that even the class jerk was impressed by Mr. Chu's nutty getup.

"May the Muses inspire our learning, and may the gods smile down upon us!" Our teacher wailed on his funky-looking harp like some ancient Greek rock star. Then he struck a pose. "I sing of the immortal Greek heroes—of mighty Hercules and clever Theseus. For today, we study ancient Greece. Quick question: Who knows what tree the Greek civilization was founded upon?"

Hands shot up. "The redwood?" said Big Pete, who'd been amazed by the giant trees on his family's trip to Sequoia National Park.

Mr. Chu smacked his forehead with the back of his hand. "Alas!" he wailed. "That is incorrect. The gods weep!"

Amrita's upraised arm whipped back and forth like a palm tree in a hurricane. I knew she'd have the right answer, but we didn't get to hear it that day. Just then, our classmate José burst into the room, eyes wild, clothes rumpled, and hair sticking up at funny angles.

"Take a seat, citizen, and—" Mr. Chu began.

But José acted like he hadn't heard a word. He staggered across the front of the room, gripping his hair in two fists. I suddenly understood how he'd gotten his new hairstyle.

"Ohhh, beware!" he wailed. José's jittery eyes looked at everyone and no one. "They are here, here among us!"

Kids laughed uncertainly. Was he joking?

"Zip it, weirdo!" called Tyler Spork.

"Yeah, zip it good," echoed his sidekick, Big Pete.

"José?" said Mr. Chu, suddenly serious.

José ignored all three of them. Clawing at the front of his T-shirt, he moaned, "The horror! Oh, the horror!"

A chill dribbled like ice water down my back. Ever since Benny and I had rescued Mr. Chu from his fate as a were-hyena, we'd found more than our share of horror—real horror—in Monterrosa. And after tackling the mutant mantis lunch ladies, the two of us had even developed kind of an underground reputation as monster hunters.

This was cool, yes. But it also tended to land us in situations that risked life and limb, which was not so cool.

Benny half rose from his seat. "What horror?" he asked José. "What is it?"

Our classmate's unseeing eyes brimmed with tears. "Everyone sent back to Belize." His voice quavered. "I'm all alone. So alone."

Stepping to José's side, Mr. Chu wrapped an arm around his shoulders. "What's wrong? Has something happened to your family?"

"Gone, all gone . . ." José shook his head over and over, his voice cracking.

Mr. Chu guided our classmate toward his seat. "There, now. Just—"

"Aaiieee!" Throwing off our teacher's arm, José vaulted onto Cheyenne's desk in one bound. Pretty impressive for a guy with no gymnastics training. He shielded his head as if expecting vampire bats to burst from the ceiling.

"The monnnsters!" he keened. "They're heeerrre!"

Monsters? I thought. Not *again*.

Everyone flinched, staring up at the ceiling tiles.

And with that, José gave a low moan, swayed, and crumpled like a wall poster when the masking tape gives out.

"Catch him!" cried Tina Green.

Cheyenne squealed. But Mr. Chu snagged José before he could squash her. Cradling our classmate in his arms, he carried him back down the aisle and laid him gently on the floor beside the funky harp.

"Is he dead?" asked Big Pete, jumping to his feet. "'Cause I've never seen a dead guy. That would be cool."

Mr. Chu scowled. "You'll have to check that off your bucket list another time. He's not dead. Just unconscious."

Everybody crowded around, offering advice and trying to help. José lay still, his face slack.

"Raise his feet," said AJ. "That's what you do for shock."

"No, raise his head," said Gabi.

"Bundle him up," said Benny.

"Give him air," said Tina.

"Everyone take your seats." Mr. Chu tugged his sport coat off the back of his chair, folded it up, and slipped it under José's head. "Amrita, go get the nurse."

She spun and dashed out the door.

"What is it?" I asked. "What's wrong with him?"

Mr. Chu motioned for us to back away from José. "Too much sun," he said. "Probably got heatstroke and fainted. Everyone, sit down."

I glanced out the window at the overcast skies.

"Heatstroke?" said Benny. "In December?"

"More like monster stroke," I whispered.

Benny nodded grimly.

Despite Mr. Chu's efforts to awaken José, our classmate was out cold. He didn't even respond to a wet towel on his forehead. And when Ms. Kopek, the school nurse, showed up, her smelling salts had no effect. José was hibernating harder than a groundhog in December.

Before we knew it, Ms. Kopek had carried José to her office and phoned his parents. Mr. Chu resumed talking about the heroes and legends of ancient Greece.

"Odysseus fought in the Trojan War, then tried to sail home with his men," our teacher said. "But he had the worst luck. He kept running into mon—uh, monsters, at, uh, every turn." Mr. Chu clutched the front of his bedsheet toga and stared out the window with a haunted expression. The pause stretched.

"And?" said Tyler. "Don't stop at the good part."

Mr. Chu blinked. "Oh. Um, most fearsome of these m-monsters was the one-eyed giant Cyclops."

Was he remembering his own personal monster mania?

He gave a little shudder, the moment passed, and he went on with his talk. Class seemed back to normal.

9

But I was sure—sure as I knew that a dish called Chef's Surprise is always a surprise, but never a good one—that normal was a long ways off. Something was wrong at Monterrosa Elementary. Again.

And if the past was any indication, Benny and I would have to put it right.

Chapter Two

Boo's Clues

AH, AFTERNOON RECESS. Since we'd lost our PE teacher to budget cuts, this was our gym period, normally a time for playing tetherball and soccer, avoiding bullies, and blowing off steam. But not today. José may not have been my best friend, but when something bad happens to your classmate, you do something about it. As soon as Benny and I stepped outside, we cut through the crowd and huddled in a corner of the playground.

"Okay," said Benny, "tell me that wasn't deeply strange."

"That was deeply strange," I said.

"Our own classmate, raving and passing out?"

I nodded. "Things are getting weird again."

Benny grinned. "And when the going gets weird—"

"The weird get going," I finished. I shook my head. "I can't believe we've got another monster problem so soon."

"Lucky us."

We didn't waste time debating whether or not to take action. After twice tackling supernatural baddies at our school, putting on the hero hat was getting to be a habit for Benny and me. And we weren't the only ones.

"So," said Tina Green, popping up from nowhere, "where do we start looking for the monsters?"

"What do you mean *we*?" said Benny.

Tina scowled. She had a good scowl. "Duh. You guys plus me equals we."

Everyone called her Karate Girl, although Benny and I had learned that she'd gotten all her moves from kung fu movies rather than actual karate classes. We didn't blab about it, though—Tina could still punch harder than most boys. And she was a good person to have on your side.

"I don't remember inviting you to tag along." Benny's lips clamped together. He was in a cranky mood, for some reason.

"Benny—" I began.

"Oh, yeah, Brackman?" Tina thrust her chin forward, the movement making her beaded braids click together with a *tik-tik-tik*. "And I don't recall your complaining when I helped you take down the alpha hyena."

"Guys, guys . . ." I said.

Benny's fists landed on his hips. "And where were you when we were fighting those mantis lunch ladies? Oh, right—chasing after us and trying to eat us!"

"Not fair!" Tina said. "I was—"

"Enough!" I stepped between them, raising my hands. "Chill out—we're all on the same team."

Tina snorted. "I'm not playing on any team where I'm not wanted."

"Karate Girl, please." I reached out, but she turned and walked off.

She called back to us, "See if I lend a hand when you get carried off by giant vampire chickens."

I wheeled on Benny. "That was rude. She was trying to help."

"We don't need her. *We're* the heroes here."

"But Tina—"

Benny tugged my arm. "Are we going to waste our recess yakking, or are we going to find out what happened to José? Let's go, Carlos. *Chop-chop!*" And he marched off without a backward glance.

I sighed and followed him. When Benny gets in his bossy mood, sometimes it's easiest to just go along. But the way he treated Tina gave my gut a twinge. It's no fun being in the middle when your friends fight.

After asking around, Benny and I learned that José was last seen at lunchtime, near the portables. (I've always wondered why they call those big temporary classrooms portables. They're about as portable as a beached blue whale.)

The classrooms would've been locked at lunchtime,

so we knew José hadn't been inside. We circled around the buildings searching for clues. Benny and I pored over the ground like my dog, Zeppo, when he's hunting for a dropped tortilla chip.

"What exactly are we looking for?" I said.

Benny flapped a hand vaguely. "Anything suspicious. We'll know it when we see it."

Hands on knees, I squinted down at some torn candy wrappers. Suspicious? Only if some kid had managed to save his Halloween candy for over a month—that's supernatural self-control.

Suddenly, out of nowhere, a spiked stick lanced down and speared the trash. I gave an involuntary cry, tumbling backward. Were we under attack?

"Dudes," said a familiar raspy voice. I relaxed. It was the head custodian, Mr. "Malibu" Decker, known to most kids as Mr. Boo. He looked like a cross between a blond Wookiee and an unmade bed. Just then he was on trash patrol.

"Hey, Mr. Boo," I said. "Did you hear about José?"

He nodded his shaggy head. "Major bummer, dude. He's in the hospital, and they're saying he's in a coma."

A coma?! Benny and I traded a wide-eyed look. This had gotten serious fast.

"We're trying to figure out what happened to him," said Benny.

"And this is the last place he was seen before he flipped out," I added. "Any idea what might have caused it?"

Mr. Boo scratched his head, scrunching up his face. "Some dudes are allergic to bees and stuff. Maybe he got stung by a bee? Or bitten by a spider?"

"The only things José's allergic to are peanut butter and homework," said Benny.

The lanky custodian planted his stick and leaned on it. "I hear you on that. It's like Michael Jackson said: 'Beat it, beat it, no one wants to eat a peanut.'"

"Uh, right," I said. "But José just gets a rash and a runny nose from peanut butter. I've never heard of it putting someone into a coma."

"It's a mystery, all right," Mr. Boo agreed. "And here's another one. Look what I spotted." He lifted his stick and pointed it at some tracks in the mud.

"What's this, itty-bitty puddles?" said Benny, who wasn't the outdoorsiest guy around.

"Animal tracks?" I guessed.

Mr. Boo nodded. "Feral cats."

"What are Will Ferrell's pets doing here?" said Benny.

"*Feral* means 'wild,'" said Mr. Boo. "And these cats are pretty big ones, by the looks of it."

"Yeah, so?" Benny tapped his foot.

The janitor looked hurt. "You dudes like weirdness. I thought you'd be interested."

"I don't think a kitty is what we're after," said Benny. "Unless cat allergies put José into a coma."

"Doubtful," said Mr. Boo.

"We're looking for something *really* unusual," I said. "José was raving about monsters just before he fainted. Seen any monsters around?"

"Yeah, like were-pandas, mutant stinkbugs, that kind of thing?" Benny added.

Mr. Boo rubbed his cheek. "Not lately. Not since the exterminator came and—"

The bell rang, and that put an end to that. After getting the custodian's promise to keep us posted on any further oddness, Benny and I headed back to our room.

"You know," I said, "mystery solving would be a lot easier without all these pesky classes."

"Tell me about it," said Benny.

"After all, it's not like we ever learned anything important in the classroom."

There should be some kind of smartphone app that warns us when we say something boneheaded.

Because I didn't know it yet, but I was wrong. Dead wrong.

Chapter Three

Just Ghost to Show You

THE STRANGENESS STARTED not far into the next period. Mr. Chu was reading us *Holes*—which, if you haven't read it, is an awesome book when the moaning began.

He glanced up from the page. "Tyler, if you don't like the story, at least keep quiet for those who are listening."

Tyler Spork held up both hands. "Wasn't me." And from the surprised expression on his face, he actually seemed to be telling the truth.

With a skeptical grunt, Mr. Chu resumed his reading. Not a minute later, another moan rang out, this one louder than the first.

Mr. Chu scowled. "If you can't be more mature, I'll stop reading right now."

"Nooo!" cried the class.

Cheyenne raised her hand. When Mr. Chu called on her, she said, "I think the noise is coming from over here." She pointed to the heating vents, low on the wall beside her desk.

The other kids in her row—Jackson, Hannah, and a new student named Esme—all leaned toward the wall, listening. For a little while, nothing happened. Then, just as Mr. Chu started to speak, another moan welled up. It sounded creepy, like a cross between an evil spirit and a dog with tummy trouble.

Jackson crinkled his nose. "Eew, it smells kind of funky over here."

"Maybe you shouldn't have had the bean burritos for lunch," said Big Pete, with a laugh. Tyler cackled and reached across the aisle to bump fists.

"Settle down, gentlemen," said Mr. Chu. He was way too polite; *gentlemen* describes Pete and Tyler like *short stuff* describes LeBron James. Our teacher slipped a bookmark into the book, then rose and approached the funky side of the room.

His nostrils flared. "Whoa now! It *does* smell funny over here. Does anyone have a moldy sandwich in their desk?" Heads shook no. "A sick wombat?" By then a whiff of the smell had reached my row. *Funny* was putting it mildly— the stench was a mix of wet cat, moldy sweat socks, and rancid cheese. Lucky thing it was faint, or we would've had to abandon the classroom.

The new girl, Esme, slumped in her chair. "We're in for it now."

"What do you mean?" asked Jackson.

"Isn't it obvious?" she said.

"What?" said Benny.

"Moans and strange smells are two signs of a haunting."

Several kids bit their fingernails. Benny twisted the front of his T-shirt.

Tyler scoffed. "Right. Our school is haunted."

"By the ghost of some kid who died from a bean burrito overdose!" Big Pete giggled. He was really working that joke.

"Or by the ghost of Simon Jenkins," said Mr. Chu quietly.

Benny blanched. "Who's Simon Jenkins?"

Casting his gaze over the class to make sure everyone was listening, Mr. Chu said, "It happened just before I came here. Poor kid. He died of fright . . . from a pop quiz!"

Several of my classmates groaned.

Mr. Chu shushed them. "Now, I'm sure the smell isn't from anything supernatural. Probably just some critter that crawled into the heating system and got stuck."

Hannah shivered suddenly, and Esme noticed.

"Cold spots," she said. "Another sign of a spirit presence." Her eyes were as big and dark as a pair of plums in yogurt.

"Also the sign of an open window," Benny muttered. But his joke sounded hollow. I knew for a fact that the whole idea of ghosts weirded him out.

"My uncle stayed in a haunted house once," said Tina Green. "He still has nightmares to this day."

Several kids fidgeted in their seats. Cheyenne twisted a lock of her hair.

"Like I said, I'm sure it's—" Mr. Chu began.

"My grandma saw ghosts in Hawaii—the Night Marchers," said Zizi Lee. "It turned her hair all white."

"Ooh," said several of her friends.

Esme looked gloomier than a Monday in January. "It's hard to get rid of ghosts. Sometimes even priests can't help."

"How come you know so much about it?" I asked.

"Yeah," said Tyler. "What makes you the expert?"

Esme gave him a slow blink, and I noticed her dark mascara. An odd choice for a fourth grader, but it matched her black jeans and black T-shirt, which read I LIKE YOU! I'LL EAT YOU LAST.

"My mother makes monsters," she said, "so I should know."

Tyler snorted. "Riiight."

"We, uh, already covered monsters before recess," said Mr. Chu, looking a bit rattled. "Remember the Gorgon!" I guessed he found the idea of someone being in the monster biz a wee bit unsettling. Fancy that.

Benny's gaze met mine. This info about Esme's mom was news—assuming Esme wasn't a wannabe Goth who liked to make stuff up. I promised myself to look into it soon.

"What kind of monsters?" Tina asked Esme.

"The drudge-asaurus," said our teacher. "It hides under your bed and eats all the books you don't want to read."

"Huh?" said Tina.

"That's not a real—" Tyler began.

Clapping his hands, Mr. Chu said, "All right now. Enough ghosts and ghoulies. I'll talk to Mr. Decker, and I'm sure he'll take care of the situation. In the meantime, let's try to ignore the poor critter in the ducts and get back to Stanley Yelnats."

He picked up *Holes* and resumed reading. And after jumping at a few last moans, my jittery classmates finally settled down to listen.

But I still couldn't concentrate. I wondered: (a) what connection did Esme have to whatever had moved into our school? (b) could it really be a ghost? and (c) if so, could a ghost have caused José's freak-out and coma?

Like a student who forgot to do the homework, I didn't have any answers. But I did know where to start looking for them, and I vowed to go there with Benny right after school.

If downtown Monterrosa were a hipster's head, then Amazing Fred's Comix and More would be the cool hat that topped it. Located just off of Main Street in a funky green-and-black building, it was packed with enough comics, games, and magic supplies to eat up a hundred lifetimes' worth of allowance money.

As soon as Benny and I pushed open the door, a speaker deep inside the store played the first four bars of the *Indiana Jones* theme. Like always, it made me feel a teeny bit more heroic.

"Hey, it's my two favorite customers," said Mrs. Tamasese, the owner. She swiveled her tricked-out purple wheelchair around from where she'd been working on a female superheroes display. "Howzit, boys!"

"Hey, Mrs. T," Benny called.

She was the most famous person I'd ever met—much more so than my bratty little sister, Veronica, who had a role on a Disney Channel series. Veronica had only been on that show for a month. But Mrs. Tamasese had ruled the WOW (Women of Wrestling) circuit for years as the Samoan Slammer, until an accident landed her in that chair.

"We just got the newest Spider-Man, Carlos." Mrs. Tamasese grinned. "Ho, that bugger bit off more than he can chew this time!" She tended to talk about superheroes like they were old wrestling buddies.

"Can't wait," I said. "But first—"

Mrs. T held up a powerful hand. "Let me guess. Things are getting freaky at Monterrosa Elementary again?" Not only was she a comic-book wizard, but Mrs. Tamasese was also our go-to expert on the supernatural.

"Wow, it's like you're psychic," Benny said.

"Psycho, maybe." She made a goofy face.

Then her expression grew serious. Mrs. Tamasese glanced right and left, motioning us to join her in a quieter part of the store. "This monster stuff is happening more and more often. I think there's something wrong with the town."

"Well, yeah," said Benny. "Not nearly enough ice cream shops."

I elbowed him. "We noticed, too. Something's up."

Mrs. T leaned forward. "So what is it this time? Were-panthers? Giant spiders?"

"We're not sure," I said. "Maybe ghosts."

Benny gave an involuntary shudder. "It all started this morning."

We filled her in on the happenings in our classroom, and on José's coma.

"Geez, poor kid." Mrs. Tamasese toyed with an earring. "I've never heard of ghosts putting someone into a coma before. But the rest does sound like the classic signs of a haunting."

Benny ran a shaky hand through his hair. "Really? But *you* don't believe in ghosts, right?"

She shifted her brawny shoulders. "Why not? Just because we can't see something doesn't mean it isn't there. You can't see electricity either, but stick a fork in a toaster, and it'll shock your socks off."

I checked around. The nearest shoppers were out of earshot. This was good, because I felt kind of funny talking about ghosts.

"So how do we get rid of it?" I asked.

"Beats me." Mrs. T shrugged, pulling out her smartphone.

"Who you gonna call," I said, "Ghostbusters?"

The storeowner made a you're-not-as-funny-as-you-think face. "I'm looking it up online."

"Seriously?" said Benny. "I thought you said all the best supernatural info is in dusty old books."

Typing in her search word with lightning thumbs, she said, "It is. But that's no reason to turn up your nose at the Internet."

Honey Girl, her fluffy calico cat, ambled up and rubbed against Mrs. T's feet, purring. She scratched it behind the ears. "Let's see . . . okay, there's smudging. . . ."

"Like smudging a sketch?" said Benny. He shifted from foot to foot. "How do you smudge what you can't even see?"

"Nah, it means burning sage or herbs to cleanse the area," said Mrs. T.

I grimaced. "If this thing is strong enough to knock someone out, I don't think stinky smoke will drive it away."

"Or you could ask it to leave . . ." she continued.

"Yeah, that'll work," said Benny. He put on a sugary voice: "Pretty please with sugar on top, will you stop haunting our school?" His words were sarcastic, but he was biting his thumbnail.

Honey Girl leaped up onto Mrs. T's lap for more in-depth petting.

"Or you could call in the professionals," said the store owner. "A priest for an exorcism, or a medium for a séance."

Benny and I made the same skeptical face. We'd tried an exorcism on Mr. Chu when he was turning into a were-hyena, and all it got us was grief and detention. That left one choice.

"So tell us," I said. "What exactly is a séance?"

Chapter Four

Ready, Fret, Go!

AS IT TURNED OUT, Mrs. Tamasese knew a whole lot more about séances than you'd expect from a former pro wrestler. She explained that they were a way of talking to spirits and hearing their replies, through the help of a medium.

"What's a medium?" I asked, trying to lighten Benny's mood. "One size less than a large?"

Mrs. T raised an eyebrow. "Pardon me while I die laughing. It's someone who uses psychic powers to communicate between the living and the dead."

A shudder rippled through me. For a second, I kind of hoped that Monterrosa was fresh out of mediums so we wouldn't have to go through with this. But as it happened, Mrs. T knew just where to find one.

"She's a teacher at your school," said the store owner. "Jessica Freshley."

"Miss Freshley?" said Benny. "Since when is a kindergarten teacher a psychic?"

"It's true you don't need ESP to read a rugrat's mind." Mrs. Tamasese chuckled. "But she mostly uses her powers after school hours."

I scratched my head. "And, um, how do we know she's the real deal?"

"Monterrosa's a pretty small place. People tend to meet others with similar interests, and you know I know my supernatural stuff. She's real, all right."

A little color returned to Benny's face. "Okay, then," he said. "We visit her first thing tomorrow to see if she'll hold an after-school séance for us."

"Agreed," I said.

"Better clear it with your parents, and your custodian, too," said Mrs. T, stroking her cat's back. "After all, someone will have to unlock the room after hours."

"Parents and psychic, check," said Benny. "Mr. Boo, check. Anything else?"

Scanning her store, Mrs. Tamasese noticed a couple of kids with comics heading for the cash register. "Yeah, it's best to have at least five people at the séance."

"In case the ghost challenges us to a pickup basketball game?" said Benny. You had to hand it to him—even when nervous, he kept the humor going.

She shot him with her finger. "Funny guy. No, it's something about the group energy. Makes the séance stronger."

Spinning her chair in one slick move, Mrs. T rolled off to serve her customers, broad shoulders bunching and releasing smoothly.

I walked with her a few steps. "Thanks, we'll let you know how it goes."

"You kidding? I'll be there myself," said Mrs. Tamasese. "And I'm bringing Honey Girl."

"Your cat?" I said. "Why?"

"Cats can sense the supernatural." She patted the calico. "Plus, she keeps my lap warm."

I could hardly argue with that. Benny and I said our good-byes and took off. Outside, I noticed he looked a little queasy.

"Something wrong?" I asked.

Benny gulped. "Nah," he said. "It's just . . . ghosts. Ugh."

"I know what you mean," I said.

"I really hope it doesn't turn out to be ghosts."

"If we're lucky, it won't."

Although the way *our* luck usually went, if it wasn't ghosts, it would be something much, much worse.

There may be some things that my *abuela*'s chicken enchiladas can't cure, but that list is a short one. I sat down to dinner thinking about comatose José, the mysterious new kid, and the possibility of evil spirits at my school. My muscles were tight, my breath was shallow, and my mouth was drier than a Death Valley rock garden.

But within a few bites, I felt my shoulders loosen and my breathing return to normal. Still munching, I saluted Abuelita with a forkful of enchilada and made a yummy sound.

She beamed. "I'm glad you like it. The secret ingredient is what makes it so good."

"Love?"

"Don't be silly." Abuelita chuckled. "Cocoa. Add a scoop to the sauce, and . . . *es magia*. Pure magic."

I glanced over to see if my dad was enjoying the meal as much as I was. He stared at the table, chewing like a robot, his mind a million miles away.

"Rough day, Dad?"

"Hmm?" He blinked and focused on me. "Oh, no worse than usual. Same old bits and bytes." But his smile didn't quite reach his eyes.

"Trouble at work?" I knew things could get stressful for computer programmers, whatever it was that they did.

My dad stared down at his plate, toying with his food. That's how I knew something was wrong—no one ever does anything with Abuelita's enchiladas but wolf them down.

"No, *chamaco*. I talked with your mom earlier."

I gripped the chair arm. "It's Veronica, right? Something's wrong?"

"No, your sister's fine. She loves being on the show—in fact, she wants to change her last name to Star."

That sounded like my showbiz-crazed little sister. She'd

wanted to be an actress almost from the time she could talk; she wished she lived in Gravity Falls, and she considered SpongeBob a close personal friend.

"Then what is it?" I asked.

Abuelita sent him a concerned look.

"It's just . . . hard," he said.

"What is?"

"This whole living situation. Only seeing your mom on weekends—it's tough. On everyone."

I swallowed a bite, and the enchilada turned to stone in my gullet. This was how it had started with Tyler Spork's parents. First, his mom was away all week, working in San Francisco, and coming home on weekends. And then one day . . . she never came back.

My mom and sister spent every Monday to Friday down in L.A. so Veronica could do her TV show. Was this the beginning of a split? Could my own parents be headed for . . . ? I couldn't even say the word in my mind.

My hands got tingly. My throat felt tighter than a boa's embrace.

Abuelita reached across and brushed my hair back. "You okay, *mijo*? You look pale."

I didn't want to say anything about anything. Sometimes speaking your fears aloud can make them real.

"I'm fine," I muttered. But then I couldn't help turning to Dad. "Are you and Mom okay?"

He scoffed, waving his hand. "Of course. Everything's

fine. Their Christmas break is coming up next week, and we'll all be together again before you know it."

But the sadness in his eyes told me the truth.

Everything wasn't fine. And if the situation didn't change soon, I'd have more in common with Tyler Spork than I cared to admit.

Chapter Five

Freshley
Squeezed

DARK AND BROODING? Gaunt and mysterious? I had no idea what psychic mediums were supposed to look like. I only knew that they weren't supposed to look like Miss Freshley.

The next morning before class started, the tiny teacher greeted Benny and me at her door, wearing a huge smile and a red-and-white-striped top hat tall enough to hide one of her students under. Her curly hair looked like corkscrew pasta dyed electric orange. Her overalls sported a purple dinosaur on the front.

"Hi, boys, what can I do for you?" Miss Freshley asked, simultaneously wiping one kid's nose, hugging another student, and taping artwork to the door. I'd always suspected kindergarten teachers were part octopus.

"Uh, yeah," I said. "We heard that you, uh . . ."

"Will you hold a séance for us?" asked Benny, getting right to the point.

Miss Freshley blinked in surprise, checking on her students before replying. "I try to separate my personal life and school life," she half whispered.

I could relate. That morning, I'd had to put the d-word (*divorce*, that is, not *doughnuts*) out of my mind, just so I could function at school. But Miss Freshley needn't have worried about her students overhearing our psychic talk. The little rugrats were bouncing off the walls, jamming crayons up their noses, singing gibberish songs, and doing everything but listening to her.

"It's kind of important," I said. "You know that kid who went into a coma yesterday?"

Miss Freshley clapped a hand to her rainbow-sweater-covered chest. "Oh my. That poor dear boy!"

"We—and Mrs. Tamasese—think a haunting might have caused it," said Benny. "And we need your help to talk with the, uh, ghosts and find out."

Her green eyes went as round as the wheels of the bus that go round and round. "Spirits? At our school?"

"That's our best guess," I said. "We think they're haunting the ducts."

"Oh, those poor dear ducks!" she cried.

"The, uh, heating ducts," said Benny.

"Even more reason to hold a séance," said Miss Freshley,

not missing a beat. "It'll take— Caden, those are not for eating!" She hustled into the room to rescue some alphabet blocks, then rejoined us. "I'll need to go home first for my gear. Say, four o'clock today? In the mechanical room?"

"Perfect," I said. "We'll get Mr. Boo—um, Decker—to let us in."

"And we'll bring some extra people for the whole group-energy thing," said Benny.

"Delightful!" Miss Freshley beamed, as if talking to evil spirits was like having bonbons with Barbie. "I'll see you after— Olivia, what did I say about putting graham crackers down your underpants?" And she rushed off to deal with another kindergarten emergency.

Benny and I had just enough time to visit Mr. Boo before class. Since we would have adult supervision, he agreed to let us talk to spirits in his equipment room. He's open-minded that way. The custodian also mentioned that Principal Johnson had asked him to help figure out whatever had caused José's coma. Plus he'd checked inside the heating vents as Mr. Chu asked, but he hadn't found any confused possums or lost raccoons.

That meant the problem was either ghosts or something completely unknown. Somehow, that wasn't very reassuring.

Morning lessons passed, as morning lessons do. We learned more about Hercules and other Greek heroes, and started making our own cardboard shields and helmets. We got the lowdown on the water cycle. We talked about science-fair projects. In fact, we made it all the way to break time without any more ghostly moans or strange smells.

And then recess shot that all to heck.

Out on the playground, I confronted Benny again about the way he'd treated Karate Girl yesterday. "What's up with you?" I asked. "Were you in a bad mood?"

"I just don't think we need her," he said. "She's always hanging around."

I blew out some air. "Well, yeah. Tina's a friend."

"*Your* friend, maybe." He shrugged, not meeting my eyes.

For some reason, I thought of my sister, Veronica, and how she'd flipped out when her BFF, Maya, made another friend. I glanced sidelong at my buddy. Could Benny be . . . jealous?

"You know," I said cautiously, "you're my best friend."

"Well, duh," he said. "Who else would have you?"

"And no matter how many other friends I have, you're still number one."

I caught a flash of gratitude in his eyes before he said, "What am I, a bug-eating moron? 'Course I know that."

"Okay, then." I punched his shoulder lightly.

"Okay, then." He bopped me back.

"So you're cool with me inviting Tina to the séance?"

He smirked. "Hey, if you're willing to risk the cooties . . ."

Tina wasn't hard to locate. As was often the case, she could be found strutting her stuff on the monkey bars.

Esme, Amrita, and a couple other kids from our class tried to keep up.

"Hey, Karate Girl!" I called.

Reaching the end of the bars, Tina jerked her body forward and back, gathering momentum. At the top of her swing, she let go, executed a perfect flip, and touched down in the sand. "And she sticks the landing!" she crowed. "What's up, Rivera?"

"How'd you like to go to a séance after school?" I said.

"Will there be snacks?" she asked.

"Nope," said Benny. "Just spooks."

I told her about our plans. To her credit, Tina merely nodded. "Glad you came to your senses, Brackman. Count me in."

From atop the bars, Esme watched us. She wore a black cat T-shirt that read PURR EVIL and she had on the same ridiculous amount of eyeliner as before. I wondered if her mom knew Esme was swiping her Maybelline Great Lash. I also wondered how much Esme had overheard.

But before I could find out, a yowl erupted somewhere behind us. I spun.

A third-grade girl was staggering in our direction. "Bewaarrrre!" she screamed. "They're heeere! No escape!"

Kids fled before her like cats avoiding bath time. A dark-haired girl trailed the third grader, her face tight with concern.

Staring ahead blindly, Scream Girl tripped on the

wooden sandbox border and stumbled. She careened into me, gripping my T-shirt for support.

"Horrible, horrible!" she wailed into my face. Her breath smelled like oranges.

"W-what's horrible?" I asked. Prickles erupted along my shoulders and arms. Could the ghost have struck again?

Suddenly she sagged. "Nobody came to my party, not even one person," Scream Girl whimpered. "Everyone hates me."

"Well, I'm sure if they got to know you . . ." Tina began.

And then Scream Girl's eyes rolled back in her head, she sighed, and she sprawled like a boneless chicken. I only just managed to keep her head from smacking the sandbox edge.

Now that she wasn't raving, everyone crowded around. We shook Scream Girl's shoulder and patted her cheek, but she was out cold. Just like José.

"Somebody get Mrs. Johnson!" said Benny.

Amrita took off like a roadrunner with its tail feathers on fire.

Benny's eyes met mine. He didn't have to speak. His expression said it all: *Another one?* I scanned the faces around us until I spotted Scream Girl's dark-haired friend.

"You," I said.

She pointed to herself. "Abby."

"What happened to her? Did you see?"

Abby's shoulders climbed almost up to her ears. "I

dunno. Trin was off behind there." She indicated the building that housed the mechanical room, the arts classroom, and the playground equipment storage. "I heard a scream, and she ran out like a slasher was after her."

At this cheerful thought, a chill struck the group like an ice cream headache—only a lot less sweet. The kids around us watched the building uneasily.

Tina's eyes narrowed. "I don't like the looks of this."

"Oh, really?" said Benny sarcastically. "I thought it was right up there with pony rides, fuzzy slippers, and frozen Snickers bars."

She glared, and he stuck his tongue out.

"Um, girl in coma here," I said. "Hello?"

Benny cleared his throat and turned away. Karate Girl busied herself fussing over the unconscious Trin.

"Is she gonna be okay?" asked Abby, her face whiter than a sheep in a snowstorm.

"Sure, she—" Tina began.

"Not if she was ghost-touched," said Esme.

"What do you mean?" I asked.

"Her spirit will wander off, never to return."

Abby stifled a sob.

I glared at Esme. "Great bedside manner."

"Hey"—she turned up her palms—"I'm honest. If it's a ghost, nobody's safe."

The kids around me murmured to each other and drifted

away, eyeing the mechanical room. The unconscious girl was completely forgotten.

"Way to cause a schoolwide panic," said Benny.

"The truth will set you free," said Esme. "But first, it'll tick you off."

Tina snorted. "I bet you don't get invited to a lot of parties."

"Why no," said the new girl, considering, "I don't."

Parties . . . That reminded me of what Trin had said. *Nobody came to my party.* It didn't make any sense. Why . . . ?

Just then, Mrs. Johnson arrived, trailed by Ms. Kopek, the school nurse. After shooing the four of us away, they lifted Trin onto a stretcher and carried her toward the office.

"This school is kind of different," said Esme, watching them go.

"Girl," said Tina, "you have no idea."

A Froggy Day

I'M NOT QUITE SURE what I expected after a recess like that, but it definitely wasn't a lunchtime rain of mutant frogs. Word had spread rapidly about Trin's freak-out, and my classmates were as twitchy as a traffic cop on an anthill. Between our nervous chatter and the sporadic moans from the vents, it was all Mr. Chu could do to get us to focus on fractions.

An unexpected PA announcement did nothing to settle our nerves.

"Attention, all students," Mrs. Johnson's voice buzzed from the tinny speakers on the wall. "Until further notice, we will be observing the buddy system."

Frowns greeted this news. "What buddy system?" muttered Tyler Spork, probably because he'd never had, strictly speaking, any buddies. (Big Pete didn't count. He was more like a pet.)

"Whenever you're outside the classroom, stick with at least one fellow classmate at all times," our principal continued. "That means at recess, at lunch, on bathroom breaks, before and after school. Nobody is to be alone—not a single, solitary, blessed soul. Understood?"

Even though she couldn't hear us, many kids said, "Understood." Such is principal power.

"We are working on solving our . . . unusual situation here at Monterrosa Elementary," said Mrs. Johnson. "And until we do, your safety comes first."

Unusual situation? A pizza party in the principal's office was an unusual situation. This? Words could barely describe how weird it was. The room buzzed with my classmates' concern.

"Not to worry," said Mr. Chu. "Mrs. Johnson's actually doing you all a favor."

"A favor?" asked Gabi.

"Sure." Mr. Chu chuckled, but his humor didn't quite reach his eyes. "Who doesn't want to spend more time with their buddies, right?"

"Right," I said.

You had to hand it to the guy. Despite his own worries about monsters, he was trying to make this easier on us.

Then and there, Mr. Chu divided us into buddy pairs. Naturally, Benny and I were together, which suited me fine. But I don't think Tina was nearly as pleased to be stuck with Miss Mini-Goth herself, Esme Ygorre.

"Don't we get a choice?" she asked Mr. Chu.

"Not when safety's at stake," he said.

Tina scowled. "Safety is overrated."

Lunch brought little relief. Pairs of kids huddled over their trays like prison inmates, shooting jittery looks around the cafeteria. It was like they thought the Ghost of Lasagnas Past was coming for them any minute. And maybe it was.

I had my own worries to add to the mix. I couldn't stop thinking about my mom and dad, wondering whether they were discussing divorce. And if they did split, would Veronica and I go with Mom, or would one kid go with each parent? The mere thought of all this made my corn dog harder to choke down than a concrete casserole.

But at last, Benny and I finished our lunch, dropped our trays on the stack, and headed out to nose around. Aside from the edgy mood, it seemed like the same old playground. Knots of kids were doing regular kid stuff—talking, climbing the jungle gym, playing basketball and tetherball.

And then, halfway across the blacktop, the weirdness factor bumped up another notch. Just ahead of us, Amrita and Cheyenne squealed, hunching their shoulders like they were warding off blows. But there was nothing there.

Amrita turned and glared at Benny and me. "Quit it," she said.

"Quit what?" asked Benny.

Cheyenne flinched again, as if something had struck her shoulder. "It's not funny!"

"What's not?" I asked.

"Stop throwing things at us!" snapped Amrita.

Mystified, I glanced over at Benny. "We're not," we said together, holding out our empty hands.

A thought occurred to me, and I gripped his arm, watching the two girls closely. Was this the ghost at work? Were we facing a poltergeist, a spirit that could actually be felt in the physical world?

"Oh, don't deny—" Amrita began. Then, *plop!* Something small and dark ricocheted off her forehead.

Cheyenne registered that we hadn't moved. "If you're not throwing it," she said, "then who . . . ?"

Something squishy struck my cheek and rebounded. "Hey, knock it off!" I spun, searching for the prankster. But if someone was throwing things, they were better hidden than the softer side of Darth Vader. Could the ghost be doing this?

Something bounced off Benny's head. He clenched his fists and whirled. "All right, smarty-pants. Show yourself!" But no one showed.

Hands on knees, I tracked the object, squinting down at a greenish lump a bit smaller than an Oreo cookie. Was it a toy? I reached down, and then, the thing moved.

I snatched my hand back. "What the what?"

"What is it?" asked Benny.

"I'm not sure." Bending lower, I eyeballed the thing, which gave a feeble hop. "Aw, it's a little bitty frog." I extended a gentle finger to stroke it. The creature bared sharp teeth in a rodentlike head and chomped down.

"Yow!" I flicked the thing away.

"It bit you?" said Benny.

I sucked on my sore finger. "With its little mouse teeth."

Benny scrunched up his face. "Say that again?"

But then, with a pitter and a patter, the sky was raining tiny mouse-headed frogs.

"Ow! Yow!" Benny and I hunched, raising our arms for defense. One of the creatures landed in the folds of my sweatshirt and nipped me on the neck. Swatting it off, I raised my hood for protection. (Probably not the advertising slogan its manufacturers had intended—*Protects from light rain and the occasional amphibian shower.*)

Kids across the playground shrieked and scattered as the bizarro storm struck. Most ran for the shelter of trees or nearby buildings. Benny and I hustled over to the closest covered hallway, right behind Amrita and Cheyenne.

There we took cover, watching the other kids flee the froggy rain.

"Unbelievable," said Cheyenne.

"Cool!" said Benny.

"Freaky," I agreed.

"Ick!" Amrita batted at her hair. "Are they gone?"

Cheyenne assured her she was critter-free—which was

more than I could say for the students stuck on the playground. Several kids had frozen under pressure, curling into the fetal position and getting hammered by the tiny creatures. I wanted to help them (the kids, that is), but I didn't want to be bitten by any more of them (the frogmice). We yelled at the students to run.

Strangely enough, Big Pete actually dashed *into* the downfall, holding out a plastic wastebasket and chortling. From where we stood, I could just make out his cry of "Sweet science-fair project!" as he collected mutant amphibians from the sky.

Then, as suddenly as it had begun, the froggy rain slowed to a light shower, then a drizzle. Finally, only the odd *plop* and *ribbit* here and there. Pete scooped a bunch more frogs into his bin, then hurried off to examine his windfall. The whole school smelled like an aquarium desperately in need of a cleaning.

"That was different," said Benny.

"You think?" I said.

"I've heard of pennies from heaven, but frogs?"

I scratched my head. "What could have caused it? Could it be connected to the haunting?"

"It's a curse!" Cheyenne's voice startled me.

"What now?" I edged back. Was she about to start raving and pass out like José and Trin?

Cheyenne clutched her jacket together and stared across the moving carpet of mutant amphibians. "Like in the Bible.

It's a plague on our school—we're being cursed!"

"That's ridiculous," Benny scoffed.

"No, it's not," said Amrita.

Shaking her head, Cheyenne mumbled, "First, the kids going into comas; now this."

I stepped closer to her. "But it wasn't a curse that made those kids zap out. It was . . ."

"What?" said Cheyenne.

"We're, um, working on finding out," I said. Probably best not to mention ghosts when she was in this kind of mood.

Cheyenne brushed me aside. "I know what I know. Let's go, Amrita." She strode up the hallway.

"Where are we going?" her friend asked, trailing after.

"To transfer to another school. This one's not safe."

Benny and I watched them leave.

"Can't argue with that," I said, rubbing my sore neck. "Most schools, you don't get bitten just walking across the blacktop."

He waved it off. "Let's leave the frice to Mr. Boo. We've gotta stay focused on the ghost."

"Frice?" I said.

Benny lifted a shoulder. "Frog-mice—frice."

I raised my eyebrows. "Really?"

"What would you call them," he said, "mogs?"

"Call them what you like," I said. "Just don't ask me to clean them up."

Chapter Seven

The Blair Rich Project

I N THE BEST of all possible worlds, school would've been canceled after an event like that, which would let Benny and me do our séance early and go home. But three things told me Monterrosa Elementary wasn't in the best of all possible worlds.

First, classes continued (in fact, Mr. Chu even tried to turn the frice into a science lesson). Second, we had to skip our afternoon recess and stay indoors, where it was "safer." And third, instead of doing something fun, like watching cartoons, we had to go to an assembly. (I suspected the assembly was the whole reason Principal Johnson hadn't canceled school.)

As our class shuffled like a chain gang down the covered walkways, Mr. Chu kept glancing out at the sky as if he expected a rain of raccoons next. Big kids were jumpy. Little kids were whiny. And they weren't the only ones.

"Why waste a perfectly good break time listening to some old dude?" Benny complained to the world at large.

"This old dude isn't just any old dude," said AJ, behind us.

"Oh no?" said Benny.

Tina Green nodded sagely. "Haruki Hanzomon is one of the richest guys on the planet. And if he wants to say something, I want to listen."

Benny grunted. "I'd still rather be watching *Samurai Jack*." But I suspected he was curious.

We filed into the multipurpose room, joining all the other classes already sitting on the cold tile floor. As the last groups took their seats, I watched the screen. A computer-animated piece was playing: a spinning globe with plants on it that morphed into heavy construction equipment, which evolved into buildings, which turned into computers, and finally transformed into a sparkling sky-blue logo that read HANZOMON INTERNATIONAL.

I nudged Benny. "Judging by that, you'd think they make almost everything on the planet."

"Who says they don't?" he said.

At last, everyone got settled and Mrs. Johnson introduced our guest. I'll admit I spaced out on the first few things she said, because my busy mind was spinning various scenarios about how our after-school séance would go from mild catastrophe to total disaster.

But when our principal said something about a "special relationship," it caught my attention.

"Today's guest has offered to underwrite our school's science program," said Mrs. Johnson. Her brown eyes sparkled like this was the principal's equivalent of getting a BMX bike on Christmas morning. And maybe it was. "To start out, he's sponsoring this year's science fair, and providing brand-new tablet computers for every student in grades four through six."

The room erupted in cheers from the upper grades and groans from the lower ones. Benny elbowed me. "I like this dude already, and I haven't even met him."

Beneath all the noise, it sounded like Mrs. Johnson was saying, "Please welcome Mr. Handybum!" But I suspected the guy's name was actually Hanzomon, like Tina had said. Just call me Mr. Perceptive.

Trumpets blasted a fanfare fit for some old-timey king, drowning out the chatter with sheer volume. Slowly, the red velvet curtains parted, and a dark-suited figure strode onto the stage.

He wasn't particularly tall. He wasn't young or old. In fact, he wasn't especially memorable in any way. But still the man commanded the attention of everyone in the room.

Mr. Hanzomon paced to the microphone and struck a pose with his fists on his hips. He looked like a well-dressed executive playing at Superman, but nobody laughed.

"We need new heroes," he said with a heavy Japanese

accent. "Where are the Einsteins, the Edisons, the Curies of tomorrow?"

"He wants curry?" whispered Benny. "Take him to Delhi Delight. Problem solved."

Tina thwacked the back of his head. "That's *Madame* Curie, you eggplant."

"New heroes of science need help and encouragement if they are to emerge," said Mr. Hanzomon, "and that's why I'm here today." Behind him, the screen showed tablet computers magically flying into kids' hands, students working on science projects, and the most Hollywood-ified science fair you could imagine.

Kids went *oooh*. The billionaire said something about his biotech research and how he was always searching for the "next big thing."

"Great," Benny said. "Let's take him those frice, patent them, and get rich!"

On his other side, Gabi swatted him. "Shh!"

Our visitor kept it short. Mr. Hanzomon wished us the best of luck with our science-fair projects, told us we'd be seeing a lot more of him, and closed by making one last call for the "science heroes of tomorrow!"

As we trooped out of the assembly and down the hall, I noticed a big truck with the Hanzomon International logo parked on the blacktop. A team of people in sky-blue jumpsuits was collecting the mutant frogs. One of them was arguing with Mr. Boo.

"Dang," said Benny. "They beat us to the frice."

"Mr. Boo doesn't look too happy about it," I said.

"Maybe he's territorial," said Benny. "Janitors can be that way."

But I didn't waste much time thinking about custodians and freaky frogs. Benny and I had bigger tortillas to fry. Supernatural ones, at that.

Somehow we made it through the next two hours. After class ended, I called my *abuela* and told her I'd be staying late for an after-school project. (Not a complete fib.) Tina and Benny used similar excuses, and so 3:45 found us fidgeting outside the mechanical room, waiting for the grown-ups to arrive.

The butterflies in my stomach were joined by hummingbirds. I couldn't stop worrying about all the ways this séance could go wrong: (a) What if the ghosts didn't want to talk? (b) What if they attacked us instead? And (c) What if we opened a pathway to a dark dimension and demons came boogieing down it?

(Okay, safe to say, I probably shouldn't have watched *Evil Dead* the night before. But I thought I was doing research.)

Mrs. Tamasese showed up first, hot-rodding down the hall in her souped-up purple wheelchair and black satin warm-up jacket. Honey Girl was a boneless calico-colored sprawl in her lap. I guessed the cat was used to her crazy driving.

Skidding to a stop beside us, Mrs. T offered a huge grin. "Howzit, kids!"

"You look cheerful," I said.

Her cocoa-brown eyes twinkled. "And why not? Séances are totally *da kine*—a blast."

"Yeah?" said Tina.

"For reals," said the former wrestler. "Haven't been to one since that time in New Orleans when the ghosts got so ticked off, they almost burned the house down. We had to escape out the recycling chute. Hoo-ee!"

Benny's smile was as queasy as a mountain goat going windsurfing. "Heh. Good times."

"Now, where's our medium?" asked Mrs. T. "I'm hoping she can top my last séance."

Benny's face went a whiter shade of pale. He opened his mouth, and I had a strong feeling his next words would be, *This isn't such a hot idea*. But then, something he saw shut him up.

I turned.

Striding down the hall in a tie-dyed robe, blue jeans, a princess crown, and a yellow Pokémon T-shirt came Miss Freshley herself. She plopped an oversize canvas bag onto the cement and straightened her tiara.

"Alrighty, then," said the medium, "who's ready to speak with some spooks?"

Chapter Eight

Séance, Schméance

THE MECHANICAL ROOM was as comfy and inviting as a concrete crypt at midnight. Mr. Boo had thoughtfully stacked five folding chairs and a card table in the middle of the room, for that homey touch.

Still, I didn't plan on moving in anytime soon.

Water heaters, boilers, and other mysterious machines ringed the space, sending ducts and pipes shooting out in all directions, like the legs of enormous spiders. The room smelled of mildew and oil, and a strong wet-cat-and-cabbage stink, which Honey Girl didn't like. She growled low in her throat when she entered, crouching on Mrs. Tamasese's lap.

Our medium stood in the center of the room with her eyes closed and arms extended. Seeing this, Tina lifted her eyebrows at me. I shrugged.

Miss Freshley took a deep breath. "Ah, I feel it," she said. "The spiritual emanations are strong here."

"As is the funkiness factor," said Benny, wrinkling his nose. He was trying to keep up his usual wisecracking bravado. But only someone who knew him well, like me, could spot the rigid shoulders and clenched jaw that hinted at his true feelings.

"Please," said Miss Freshley, "some respect for the spirits. Respect is a building block of character, right, boys and girls?"

We mumbled agreement. I guess you can take the teacher out of the kindergarten, but not the kindergarten out of the teacher.

She told us how to set things up. We ringed the table with four chairs, leaving a blank space for Mrs. T's wheelchair. Then Miss Freshley produced a sapphire-blue cloth from her bag and flung it over the table with a dramatic gesture. Lit candles anchored it at the four corners, and ringed the whole setup.

"For protection?" asked Tina.

Miss Freshley beamed. "For illumination." She flicked off the harsh fluorescent lights, and the room was bathed in a warm glow. Unfortunately, this glow didn't reach far. Deep shadows surrounded us, just when we were about to talk with ghosts.

I gulped.

"There, that's better," said the medium. She set a clear plastic bowl in the table's center, then added some bread, white flowers, and Hershey's Kisses to it.

"Snack time?" I asked.

Dimples bloomed in Miss Freshley's cheeks as she wagged her head. "An offering to attract our ghostly visitors."

"But, candy?" said Tina.

Mrs. T arched an eyebrow. "Living, dead, or in between," she said, "everybody loves chocolate."

I had to agree with her on that one.

"But no milk or soda?" said Benny. "Won't the spirit need something to wash it down with?"

Miss Freshley cleared her throat, sending him the kind of look that made kindergartners quail. "Will everyone please take a seat and join hands?"

We followed her instructions. Honey Girl jumped off Mrs. T's lap, circled once around the table, and hopped back up to her perch, for whatever reason cats do anything. I found myself sitting between Benny and Tina. As I reached out for her hand, I said, "This is *only* for the séance. It doesn't count as holding hands or anything. Right?"

Tina rolled her eyes. "Well, duh. Who'd want you as a boyfriend, Rivera? Cootie Central."

Reassured, I gripped her fingers. On the other side, Benny's hand felt sweaty. I gave it a little squeeze. His answering grin was as weak as a baby bird's bluster.

"Take a deep breath, everyone, and let it out," said Miss Freshley.

I must have looked worried myself, because from across the table, Mrs. T winked encouragingly.

"Now what?" said Tina.

"Now we ask for protection," said Miss Freshley. Her leaf-green eyes were huge and serious as she raised her gaze. "O Great Spirit, we seek the blessing and shelter of your white light today. Surround us all and keep us safe."

"Um, amen?" said Tina.

"Right on," said Mrs. Tamasese.

In a warm rush of feeling, I was glad she was there. Somehow, having an ex-wrestler in the room felt safer than a hundred chandeliers' worth of white light.

"And now," said Miss Freshley, "we stay as calm and happy as a hen on its nest while we invite the spirits to appear."

She went quiet. I wasn't quite sure what was called for, so I said, "Heeere, ghostie, ghostie. Niiice ghostie."

Miss Freshley's eyes narrowed. "*Mentally* invite them."

Oops.

"*I* will speak the incantation," said the medium.

Tina sent me a sympathetic wince.

"O Spirits of the Past," crooned Miss Freshley in a hollow voice, "move among us in the here and now. Come visit us in this place."

Something growled. We all tensed, but it was Benny's belly. "Sorry," he said.

The redheaded medium glared at the two of us. "Honestly, if you can't respect the process—"

"We'll be good!" I said.

"It's my usual snack time," said Benny.

She held our gaze for a few moments longer, gave a nod, and lowered her head. "Come visit us, spirits, and let us know your mind."

The silence stretched.

A deep humming sounded from the shadows. I gasped.

Goose bumps sprouted along my arms like a miniature map of the Rockies.

"The water heater," murmured Mrs. T.

I tried to breathe normally. "Of course."

"O Spirits of the Past," continued Miss Freshley, "if you are with us now, give us a sign of your presence."

Tik-tik-tik-tik! Something clicked over in the corner.

A ghost?

Benny gripped my hand like he was trying to throttle a ferret. I clenched my jaw to keep from shouting.

With a low yowl, Honey Girl flattened her ears. Either she'd eaten some bad tuna, or something supernatural was brewing.

"Yesss!" cried Miss Freshley, closing her eyes and lifting her face. "Welcome, spirits. We seek answers to our questions. I offer myself as your vehicle—speak through me!"

A faint moan seemed to rise from everywhere and nowhere. Our circle traded excited glances. It was working—the séance was really working!

Miss Freshley stood, still holding hands with Benny and Mrs. T. "We ask of you, why do you haunt us? Why have you put our students into a coma?"

The moaning swelled, sounding much like it had in my classroom. The temperature seemed to drop a few degrees. I shivered. Like a storm about to break, the pressure in the room built.

Honey Girl rose stiff-legged from Mrs. T's lap. Her eyes

were yellow moons, and her fur stood on end, like a porcupine with the frizzies. The cat produced a moan of her own.

Linking Benny's hand with Mrs. Tamasese's, Miss Freshley left our circle. Mrs. T frowned and shook her head, but the medium indicated we should keep our hands clasped. She stepped away from the table.

"Use my voice as your voice," she said, wandering through the room. "Speak your answers through me. Why have you appeared? What do you seek? Speak, O Spirits!"

She paced outside the ring of candles, closer to the shadows.

And just like that, three things happened, almost simultaneously.

First, the outside door creaked open, letting in a cool gust. Second, the candles blew out, leaving us in the dark, and third . . .

"Aaaah!" Miss Freshley screamed.

Chapter Nine

Medium, Well Done

ALL WAS DARKNESS and confusion. I felt my hands gripped tightly. The table jostled and rocked as everybody spoke over one another.

"The ghost!" Benny gasped.

"Don't break the circle!" cried Mrs. T. "It's not safe!"

"Is Miss Freshley okay?" said Tina.

"Everything all right in there?" called Mr. Boo from the door.

"No! Yes! I don't know!" I said.

Rreeeeowww! yowled Honey Girl. A weight landed in my lap, and sharp claws dug into my thighs.

"Yow!" I cried.

For a handful of heartbeats, the chaos continued. Then,

with a click and a buzz, the fluorescent lights blinked on, revealing the custodian standing just inside the doorway.

"Why were all the lights off?" asked Mr. Boo.

"It's for—" Mrs. Tamasese began.

Miss Freshley wailed again, *"Aaiieee!"*

Everyone turned as she staggered toward us, clutching two handfuls of her tangerine-colored hair. Her crown was crooked, and her eyes were as wild as a dingo in a diner.

Séance or no séance, something was deeply wrong. My skin tingled. I jumped to my feet, dumping the cat off my lap and breaking the circle.

"What's the matter?" asked Tina.

"Terrible, terrible, most terrible!" groaned the medium.

I reached out to her. "What is?"

"Doom to you all!" roared Miss Freshley, waving her arms.

"Yup, that's pretty terrible."

"Yikes!" Benny ducked behind his chair and raised crossed index fingers, like he was warding off a vampire. "I—is this the g-ghost talking, or Miss Freshley?"

The medium clutched the back of her own chair, huffing breaths in and out as if she'd been running a marathon. In response, Honey Girl arched her spine like a Halloween cat, hissing and glaring. Mrs. T wheeled to the teacher's side, her face creased with concern.

"It's too late, it's too late, it's too late," whimpered Miss

Freshley. Her expression was heartbreaking. "They're all doomed, and I couldn't do a thing. My fault . . ."

Then, her eyes rolled back in her head. Mrs. Tamasese lunged, but too late. Miss Freshley slumped forward, collapsing her chair and doing a face-plant onto the spirit offering.

Hershey's Kisses flew everywhere.

Fwump! Down went the table, with the medium on top.

"Jessica!" Mr. Boo hurried to her side.

We all crowded around. By the time we rolled Miss Freshley over and checked her vital signs, it was obvious.

She was out like a light, and nothing could awaken her.

The ghost of Monterrosa Elementary had struck again.

With our help, Mr. Boo loaded the comatose teacher into his car and strapped her down. "Don't worry, dudes," he said. "I'll make sure she gets the best care."

My stomach was twisted up with guilt like a shopping-mall pretzel. If Benny and I hadn't brought her into this, Miss Freshley would've been home making brownies, or learning silly songs, or whatever kindergarten teachers did in their free time.

"We're coming with you," I told the janitor.

This was strongly vetoed by both Mr. Boo and Mrs. Tamasese.

"No way," he said. "You dudes need to get home. Your parents will be worried."

"But it's our fault," said Benny.

The ex-wrestler scowled. "Not even," she said. "Miss Freshley is an experienced medium; she knew the risks." Her face softened. "I'm sure she'll snap out of it soon."

"But we—" Tina began.

"Nope," said Mr. Boo. "Like the Eagles say, 'Bikes in the fast lane.' Go! We've got this covered."

He drove away, with Mrs. T following in her van. Benny, Tina, and I looked at each other, shrugged, and shuffled off to unlock our bikes. I hadn't felt quite so useless in a long while. First, my parents were careening toward a split, and now this.

The setting sun glazed the oak trees an applesauce gold, but I was in no mood to admire a sunset. Our school was falling apart—student by student, teacher by teacher. And so far, we hadn't done a darned thing to stop it. My chest felt as tight as a superhero's spandex.

"If this keeps up," Tina said as we pedaled away, "you know what'll happen?"

"What?" I said.

"The whole school will be in a coma."

"No way," said Benny. He still looked pale, but determined. "We won't let it go that far."

Tina stood on her pedals. "Brackman, you know I give you guys major respect as monster fighters. But you've never gone up against ghosts before. You can't fight what you can't touch."

With a wave, she peeled off and headed home.

"We'll find a way!" Benny called after her. But his tone held seven shades of doubt. "Spirits or no spirits, we'll put a stop to all this. Right, Carlos?"

"Right," I said. But what I wanted to say was, *How?*

Miss Freshley had tried and failed. And if a professional psychic had been beaten by this ghost's evil mojo, what chance did two fourth-grade boys stand against it?

Chapter Ten

Bad Dare Day

IF YOU MEASURE the success of school time by how much actual learning gets done, the next morning was a total washout. But if you measure it by the amount of rumors, backtalk, and misinformation, then Mr. Chu's class was a raging success.

Talk of last night's séance had spread all over school, in the mysterious way those things do. And it seemed like some strange attitude had spread with it. All morning long, kids were sending Benny and me suspicious glances. When Benny confronted AJ after our classmate's dirty look, all AJ said was, "You know what you did."

"No, what?" demanded Benny.

But AJ turned away with a scowl and said no more.

Kids were jumpier than a kangaroo rat in a rubber room. And the occasional moans and funky smells rising from the heating vents didn't help matters much.

Even mellow Mr. Chu was edgy. Instead of leading us in Multiplication Wars or other fun math games, he actually had us do problems from the boring old textbook. And more than once, while he waited for the answer to questions like "Forty-one times six hundred and two is . . . ?," I caught him staring out the window, chewing on a knuckle. You could tell how much the recent events bothered him by how often he let talk of them interfere with our lessons.

"I heard the ghost made chocolate fly through the air!" said Amrita.

"*I* heard that it flooded the mechanical room with molten lava," said Jackson.

"No way," said Lucas. "It was ghost goo."

Funny how everyone had an opinion on something none of them had seen. I caught Benny's attention and rolled my eyes.

Gabi frowned, leaning toward us. "So, you put Miss Freshley in a coma," she said. "Who's next? Mr. Chu?"

Our teacher, overhearing this, flinched slightly.

"We never—" I began.

"We didn't do anything," said Benny. "It was the ghost."

Mr. Chu cleared his throat. "And what's, um, sixty-four times eighty-seven? Anyone?"

"Of *course* it's the ghost." Ignoring our teacher, Jackson glared at Benny and me. "And all this bad stuff just *happens* to take place while you're around. Why is that?"

Tina scowled. "Hey, I was there, too."

With a sigh, Mr. Chu said, "Does anyone have a question about something we're actually studying?"

Tyler Spork raised his hand. "I do."

"Go ahead."

"What I wanna know is, why didn't the ghost attack Carlos and Benny and put them out of my misery?"

Big Pete high-fived him across the aisle. Mr. Chu shook his head.

Esme leaned back, arms crossed. "Could have told you this would happen. I know all about the supernatural."

"Really?" said Zizi.

Benny shot me a significant look. I remembered that we'd meant to investigate Esme and her mom but hadn't gotten around to it yet. Time to move that higher on the ol' to-do list.

The morning went on in this vein. Up until the bell released us for recess, it was all Mr. Chu could do to sandwich in a few factoids here and there. (By the way, recess? An awesome invention. If not for recess, we'd never get any investigating done.)

As soon as Benny and I made it out the door, we headed off to hunt for Mr. Boo. The custodian had phoned each of us last night with the news that Miss Freshley was in a coma like the others, but we hadn't seen him yet today. Maybe he'd discovered something new about the ghost. Maybe he knew where those strange rumors about us were coming from.

Unfortunately, Mr. Boo was harder to find than a sixth grader who believed in the tooth fairy. He wasn't on the playground or in the cafeteria. His office and the mechanical room were both locked.

We never did locate him. But over on the basketball courts, we found something we weren't searching for.

"Lookie-lookie," said Tyler to Big Pete, "it's the big bad ghost hunters." The two were playing a halfhearted game of Horse. "Join us."

"Maybe later," I said.

"How's never?" said Benny. "Is never good for you?"

Tyler scowled. "Come on, hotshots, play a game."

"No, thanks," said Benny. "We're busy."

Tyler tried a hook shot that bounced off the backboard. "Busy running away from spooks?"

Benny wheeled on him. "For your information, pal, we didn't run away from anything."

"Oh yeah, *buddy*?" sneered Tyler. "I heard you unleashed the forces of darkness, then let a kindergarten teacher face them for you."

"That's ridiculous," I said.

"Or maybe this is all just some big prank," said Tyler, dribbling the ball. "You're so desperate for attention."

Benny narrowed his eyes. "*A prank?* There were witnesses. We heard stuff—heck, we even smelled stuff."

"*Sure* you did," drawled Tyler. Big Pete snickered.

My ears went hot. "There's bad stuff happening at this school."

"And maybe you're behind it," said Tyler.

"We're the only ones trying to do something." Benny's face flushed redder than a tomato kissed by a strawberry.

"If you're trying to get the whole school knocked out, you're doing a great job," said Pete. He made a *hyork-hyork* sound that I guessed was his version of a superior laugh. It sounded more like a walrus choking on a Twizzler.

Tyler got up into Benny's face. "Seems to me, if you really did see something supernatural, you're afraid to tackle it on your own."

"That's a lie!" Benny snapped.

"Then why'd you bring along a whole posse yesterday?"

I spluttered. "It—it was a séance, and—"

"Séance, schmeance," said Tyler. "You're as chicken as a bucket of Extra Crispy."

"Are not," said Benny and I together.

"Then prove it!"

I caught Benny's shoulder. "Come on, we've got better things to do."

He shook me off. "No. Nobody calls me chicken." Benny glared at Tyler. "What did you have in mind?"

A wicked grin split Tyler's face. "Tonight. The mechanical room. Just you two and the ghost. No adults. I dare you."

My stomach flip-flopped like a gold-medal Olympic gymnast. Alone in that room with a ghost? The absolute last place we should be. I didn't want to end up dead to the world for who knows how long, like José and Miss Freshley. And judging by Benny's expression, neither did he.

Tyler took our common sense as fear. "Scaredy-cats, scaredy-cats, Carlos and Benny are scaredy-cats," he chanted. Big Pete joined in, and a few bystanders laughed. It's always worse with an audience.

"Are not!" Benny and I cried.

"Then spend an hour in that room tonight," said Tyler. His eyes sparkled with an evil light, if evil eyes can sparkle. "I double-dog dare you."

The playground near us went silent. The double-dog dare, as everyone knows, is the most serious dare possible. You back out on one of those, and your reputation is mud, all the way through college.

"We accept," said Benny. And if his voice quavered a little, I didn't blame him.

"Pinkie-swear," said Tyler, extending his little finger. One at a time, Benny and I entwined pinkies with him, sealing the deal. As soon as possible, we'd need to sterilize our little fingers—I hoped we wouldn't have to boil them.

"You're all witnesses," our obnoxious classmate told the onlookers. He turned to Benny and me. "And we expect photographic proof."

"Done," I said, with a confidence I didn't feel. "And when we show it, you'll have to do whatever *we* double-dog dare *you* to do."

A flicker of doubt flitted across Tyler's face. Too late—he'd already pinkie-sworn. "It's a deal."

Just then, the bell rang. Probably just as well. I didn't think we could get into much more trouble before lunch.

As so often happens, I was wrong.

Chapter Eleven

A Matter of Principal

PARTWAY THROUGH OUR LESSON on heroes and myths of ancient Greece, the class telephone rang with the message every student dreads.

"Carlos and Benny?" said Mr. Chu, hanging up the receiver.

"Yes, Mr. Chu?" we said.

"Your number's up. Please report to the principal's office."

Our classmates were sympathetic and understanding. Everyone went *Oooh!* with great glee.

"Busted!" crowed Tyler. "I *knew* you were behind all the weird stuff."

Benny gawked at our teacher. "Us?"

"Do you know any other Carloses or Bennys in this class?" said Mr. Chu. I glanced over at my friend, but he was rooted in place, just as mystified as I was. "*Now* would be nice. Mrs. Johnson has many fine qualities, but patience isn't one of them."

As eager as a prisoner approaching the hangman, we trudged down the covered corridor. Along the way, we passed a man and woman clad in sky-blue jumpsuits with the Hanzomon logo on the chest. Benny peered up at the guy.

"Hello, boys," the man said. "We're here to help coach science-fair projects."

"Uh-huh," said Benny.

I cocked my head. "Wouldn't that be an unfair advantage?"

The woman smiled. "Not if we're helping everybody."

When we reached the office, Mrs. Gomez was sitting behind the counter, eating muffins and answering phones, same as usual. Like a spider at the center of a web, secretaries read the vibes of the entire school, so if anyone knew what we were in for, it'd be Mrs. Gomez. Her smile—or frown—could tell us a lot.

When she saw Benny and me, her face went as grim as an all-kale buffet.

So much for good news.

"Mrs. Johnson's not ready for you yet," she said. "Take a seat."

We sat on the hard plastic chairs. Benny leaned over and whispered, "Now's our chance."

"What chance?" I said.

His eyes cut over to Mrs. Gomez typing on the computer. "You distract her; I'll look up Esme's address."

"Are you nuts?" I hissed. "We're already in trouble, and you want to land us in more?"

"That's the best time," he said, "when you're already *in* trouble."

But we didn't get the chance to test Benny's theory. Just then, a buzzer sounded behind the counter, and the secretary said, "She'll see you now."

We shuffled the few steps to Mrs. Johnson's office door, and I wondered why we were in for it this time. Was it because our séance put a teacher into a coma? Or was it some other trouble we'd gotten into earlier? When you visit the principal's office as often as we do, who can keep track?

Benny knocked. When we heard "Come in," we entered the room.

"Close the door," said Mrs. Johnson.

I swallowed. This wasn't good. Closed doors meant bad news.

"Would y'all please—" the principal began in her Texas twang.

"I can explain," Benny burst out. "See, we had no idea the thing was flammable."

A frown line appeared between her eyebrows. "What are you talking about?"

Backpedaling, Benny said, "Um, it depends. What are *you* talking about?"

"The fix our school has gotten itself into," said Mrs. Johnson after a pause.

I tried to quiet my suddenly queasy stomach. "Oh," I said. "That."

She gestured to the visitor chairs, and Benny and I sat. I was as confused as a goat on Astroturf. Had our principal been talking to Tyler? Did she believe all that stuff about us causing the troubles, or was something else on her mind?

"I heard about yesterday's séance," said Mrs. Johnson. "And—"

"We are *so* sorry about Miss Freshley," Benny blurted.

"It was an accident," I said.

She held up a calming hand. "I'm aware of that. And I don't hold you two responsible."

"You don't?" said Benny and I together. Relief flooded me.

"You may have been going at it like an armadillo trying to tap-dance, but I believe you were trying to help the school," she said.

"Absolutely," said Benny.

Resting her elbows on the desk, the principal tented her long fingers. "Mr. Decker told me all about it—before he was struck down, too."

"Say that again?" My hands seemed to tingle, like a bad case of pins and needles.

"But he was fine when we saw him," Benny protested.

Mrs. Johnson's lips compressed. "Last night, yes. But he came in early this morning to try to solve this problem, and . . . Mrs. Gomez found him raving down the halls."

"No!" I crumpled like a cheap tissue. What good was it trying to be a hero if you couldn't protect your friends?

"H-how is he?" Benny asked.

The principal shook her head. "Just like the rest. This is getting to be a very bad trend."

I checked Benny's expression. He looked just as stunned as I felt.

Standing up, Mrs. Johnson smoothed the front of her lime-green pantsuit. "It's a . . . ticklish situation, to say the least. Parents are worried; the superintendent is having a conniption fit. But if I bring in the police, they'd never believe me."

"Well, yeah," I said, just for something to say.

"It's getting bad," she continued. "There's even talk of shutting down the school."

I gaped. The situation was serious.

Mrs. Johnson's fists clenched. "Not *my* school, that's for darn tootin'. I promised to educate and protect my students, and that is what I will do."

"That's right!" said Benny.

The principal's eyes flashed. "I've been an educator for twenty-two years. I've faced wildfires, budget cuts, even standardized testing—and I will not let this . . . whatever-it-is drive us out. Especially not now, when our whole science program is being underwritten by Hanzomon International."

"Never give up, never surrender!" cried Benny, caught up in the moment.

My pulse was pounding, too. I was ready to draw a line in the sand, but . . . "Why are you telling this to *us*?" I asked.

She studied Benny and me for a beat. "I know that some strange and mysterious things have gone on at Monterrosa Elementary the last couple of months."

Like were-hyenas and mutant mantises? Yeah, you could say that.

"Bad things have happened," she said, eyeing Benny, "and I'm not just talking about exploding toilets."

Benny struggled to keep a "She knows!" expression from his face, and failed.

Mrs. Johnson clasped her hands. "I believe that you two have done your part to protect the school, students, and staff from these . . . troubles."

I offered a rigid grin and lifted a shoulder. "We try."

"So . . . I would like to hire you."

I blinked. "Hire?"

"Us?" said Benny.

"Yes," said the principal. "You may be fourth graders, but for some reason, you seem to know things that no one else does."

"Tell that to Mr. Chu," Benny muttered.

Mrs. Johnson continued as though she hadn't heard. "I want you two to get to the bottom of this situation and uncover the . . . whatever-it-is that's putting folks into comas." She couldn't bring herself to say "ghost."

"Um . . ." I traded looks with Benny.

"You've got to do it by the end of the science fair on Friday, or the superintendent will shut us down."

"Wow," I said.

The principal put a fist on her hip. "And here are the conditions: Don't face this threat directly."

"But—" I began.

"When things get dangerous, you leave immediately and call me," said Mrs. Johnson. "I don't want two more comas on my conscience."

"I'm with you on that," I said. Benny gave a thumbs-up.

"Is that a yes?" she asked.

Before I could speak, Benny laid his hand on my arm. "If we do this," he asked her, "what's in it for us?"

Mrs. Johnson's eyebrows lifted. "Your school doesn't close, and no more classmates are attacked. That should be enough reward."

"How about a little help in the grades department?" Benny gave his most winning smile.

"Nope," said the principal.

"Cash?" said Benny.

"Absolutely not." The principal's arms folded and her face shut down like a ski slope in summertime.

"It's oka—" I began, but Benny cut me off.

"There must be something you can offer," he said. "After all, we're sticking our necks out here."

Her stare was as flinty as the West Texas soil. Benny had gone too far. I started to speak again, and his fingers dug into my arm like talons.

"We—ow!"

"How's this?" said Mrs. Johnson. "Two get-out-of-detention-free passes for each of you."

"Deal!" said Benny.

She eyed us. "Remember: just figure out what's causing this. *I* will take it from there."

Benny gave her a two-finger salute. "Aye aye, Commander."

I frowned. "And what if we need to get into the mechanical room, or the portables?"

Mrs. Johnson stepped over to her desk, reached under the blotter, and produced a key. She held it up.

"Is that what I think it is?" said Benny reverently.

"The universal key," she said, handing it over. "Don't lose it, don't copy it, and bring it right back as soon as this is over. Understood?"

Benny and I both nodded.

"Any questions?" the principal asked.

"Since we can't keep the key, could we have *three* get-out-of-detention passes?" said Benny.

She scowled. "Don't press your luck."

Chapter Twelve

There Ghost the Neighborhood

ONE FRUSTRATING THING about ghosts is they're tricky to pin down. Though we searched through lunchtime and afternoon break, we found no trace of the spook. Nothing poked its head out of the portables and said, *"Boo!"* Nothing floated around the mechanical room dragging chains behind it.

But our time wasn't wasted. Benny and I laid plans for tonight's ghost-hunting trip and did what we could to prepare.

"You know," Benny pointed out as we locked the mechanical room behind us, "it's not every day you get a universal key just after someone dares you to enter a locked room."

"No fooling," I said.

"We're the luckiest guys at school." Benny beamed.

"Yeah, so lucky that we have to face down a ghost." I paced. "Lucky or not, we'd better deliver."

"Relax, Carlos."

"I'll relax when we solve this and everything's back to normal. Principal Johnson isn't big on failure—not when the fate of the school is at stake."

Benny had no answer for that one but a serious look.

As a safety measure, Mrs. Johnson had closed down the portables, sent those students into the library and other classrooms, and roped off the area. Nothing interfered with our search. So naturally, the ghosts were as shy as a forest fawn at a fiesta.

Worries chased each other around and around my brain. Would we survive our ghostly encounter tonight? If we failed, would our friends be stuck in a coma forever? And would Mrs. Johnson give us detention until Benny and I were old and toothless?

Since we weren't having much luck with our search, we decided to pay an after-school visit to Esme and her mom. Esme claimed to be an expert in the supernatural; maybe we could learn something from her that would keep us safe and coma-free when we tackled Tyler's dare. And we figured her mom, a so-called monster maker, might also know a thing or two about ghosts.

Benny and I headed over to my house first because that's where the good snacks were.

"Abuelita," I called as we banged through the front door, "we're ho—"

Bam! The door slammed behind us.

"*¡Ay, Carlos!*" my grandma called from the living room.

"Sorry!" One of these times I'd actually remember to close the door quietly. Probably around the time I learned to speak Ukrainian, won the lottery, and had my own spaceship.

Abuelita turned down the ska music she'd been blasting through the house. She asked about school. I gave her the highlights, leaving out the comas and hauntings. No need to worry her.

"Are you boys hungry?" she asked.

I cut off Benny before he could make a request. "No, but someone else is. Would you mind baking something we can take to a new student in our class?"

My *abuela* smiled. "*Cariño*, that's so sweet of you to make a new student feel welcome."

"Uh . . ." I couldn't quite bring myself to admit that we were only trying to see if the new student was behind the freaky happenings at school. So I said, "Ah, *de nada*."

When Benny went to the bathroom, I helped Abuelita prepare cake batter. "So, uh . . . how's Dad doing?" I asked, my mouth suddenly dry.

She glanced up from beating eggs into a mixing bowl. "Just fine. How do you mean?"

"Oh, you know." I added sugar into another bowl and

tried to calm my heartbeat. "He seemed kind of bummed about Mom and the whole . . . L.A. situation."

"*Mijo.*" Abuelita fixed me with wise eyes. A floury hand caressed my cheek. "Don't worry. This is a hard time for them, but it won't last forever. You'll see."

I wished I felt her optimism. As Benny returned, I dropped the subject. But the heaviness in my heart remained.

Before long, my *abuela* had whipped up a batch of seriously awesome cupcakes with Mexican-chocolate frosting. Of course, Benny and I had to sample one or two. Can't give away substandard treats, after all.

We packed the cupcakes into a pink cake box, added a ribbon, and set out for the Ygorres' house. Benny and I had found the address by entering Esme's phone number from our class list into a reverse directory website that his detective dad used. I wanted to brag to someone about our mad research skills but somehow managed to restrain myself.

After a ten-minute walk, we ended up in front of a tidy Spanish-style house with a red-tiled roof. A Prius with a PROUD PARENT OF AN HONOR STUDENT bumper sticker waited in the driveway. Rosebushes lined the front of the house.

It looked about as scary as a kindergartner's vampire costume.

"This is the home of someone who makes monsters?" I said.

Benny shrugged. "Even the forces of evil like a cozy crib."

I rang the doorbell. After a short wait, the door swung open.

"Yeah?" Just like at school, Esme was a study in black—black tennies, black skirt and tights, black hoodie. The only hint of color was a purple streak in her straight black hair.

"We come bearing cupcakes," said Benny, thrusting the box forward.

She raised an eyebrow. "How jolly. We're not buying any."

"No," I said, "it's a gift—kind of a welcome-to-our-school thing."

Esme frowned. Maybe she hadn't been welcomed very often.

"Who is it, honey?" called a woman's voice from inside the house.

"Boys from school," said Esme. "And cupcakes."

"Aren't you going to invite them in?"

Wordlessly, Esme padded into the house, leaving the door open. Benny and I stepped into an entryway that seemed straight from one of those pimp-your-house TV shows. The tile floor was spotless. The artwork was tasteful. The magazines on the side table had been positioned using a ruler and T-square. It looked more like a fancy hotel for robots than a home for humans.

"Welcome!" A dark-haired woman abandoned her laptop

computer in a side room and came to greet us. Her makeup was as perfect as her smile. "I'm Esme's mother, Yvonne Ygorre."

Apparently, someone had been a bit too generous with the Ys when she'd been born.

Benny and I introduced ourselves and handed her the cupcakes. After ushering us into the family room, Mrs. Ygorre went to fetch dessert plates and napkins. Esme sat at one end of a spotless tan couch, tongue peeking from a corner of her mouth as she drew on a sketch pad.

"So, uh, nice house." I took a seat at the far end of the sofa. Benny sank into an armchair.

"It's okay," she said.

Glancing over, I noticed she was shading in a particularly gruesome scene. "Nice, uh, zombie. Looks like he's really enjoying those brains."

Her dark stare was as flat and direct as a two-by-four to the face. "Why are you here?"

"To welcome you," said Benny. "You know, like friendly people do?"

Esme snorted. "Funny," she said. "No, really, why are you here?"

At that moment, Mrs. Ygorre saved us by returning with plates and cupcakes. I was already kind of full, but I made the sacrifice and ate one anyway. Politeness is my middle name. After she'd served everyone, Esme's mother perched in an armchair and cut into her treat using a knife and fork.

With her wire-rimmed glasses, casually stylish clothes, and friendly attitude, she seemed like the cool mom on a Disney Channel show.

"So," she said, "you boys are in Esme's class? She never mentions you."

"We're pretty boring," said Benny.

"Yeah," I said. "Not half as interesting as what's been going on lately."

Esme's mom took a dainty bite of cupcake. "Science-fair projects?"

"The haunting," said Benny.

Esme stayed focused on her drawing. Mrs. Ygorre patted her lips with a napkin. "Ah, yes, ghosts putting people into a coma. Esme mentioned something about that."

She seemed so calm, like we were discussing Kool-Aid choices for Parents' Night. I glanced at Benny, unsure how to proceed.

"Esme made it sound like you guys have had some experience with the supernatural," said Benny.

Our classmate snorted again, and her mom trilled a tinkling laugh. "You might say it's a family tradition," said Mrs. Ygorre.

"Huh?" I said. Yeah, I'm real smooth.

"She means our family has been working with spooks, monsters, and ghouls for over a hundred and fifty years," said Esme.

Okay, we'd expected there might be a *little* truth to Esme's claim, but not this. I don't know if my mouth fell open as far as Benny's, but his was wide enough to catch a whole swarm of flies, with room left over for a California condor.

"You, uh, what now?" I said.

"It's no secret," said Esme's mom. "Since my great-great-grandfather's day, the Ygorres have been serving scientists and . . . others."

"Others?" Benny choked out.

Mrs. Ygorre lifted a shoulder. "Certain people who experiment with the supernatural. We always say, 'Can't make a monster . . .'"

"'Without a Ygorre,'" Esme finished with her.

Just then, I had a major *duh* moment. I'd heard Esme and her mom pronounce their last name *Yuh-GOR*, with the accent on the last syllable. But I remembered a movie where someone with a similar name helped a mad scientist. . . .

"Igor," I said. "Like Frankenstein's Igor?"

Esme rolled her eyes and went back to her drawing.

Her mom tut-tutted. "That poor man," she said. "The movies were so inaccurate, it was embarrassing. They made it seem like what he did was wrong."

"Fancy that," said Benny, in a strangled tone.

She loaded another small bite of cupcake onto her fork. "So that's why we Ygorres changed the family name a bit. People just didn't understand."

"Small minds," I said, while my brain screamed, *Dr. Frankenstein and Igor were real?*

"Exactly," said Mrs. Ygorre.

Benny stared. I knew the same thought was racing through both of our minds: Was this monster-loving family behind the haunting at our school?

I munched some cupcake to give myself time to think. Then, as casually as possible, I said, "So, uh, are you carrying on the family tradition here in Monterrosa?"

Mrs. Ygorre sighed. "I was. For two weeks. But then my employer and I had some differences of opinion."

"Differences?"

Her lips pursed. "He was reckless, unprofessional, taking things too fast."

"Sloppy work produces sloppy monsters," said Benny.

"Precisely," said Mrs. Ygorre. "Plus, I found out his health benefits didn't include dental, and that's a deal breaker."

"Mm-hmm," Esme seconded, not looking up from her sketch.

My mind raced. So Mrs. Ygorre had been here only two weeks, working for some monster maker. Maybe Esme's mom wasn't behind the trouble at our school, but she might know who was.

"Who did you work for?" I asked.

Mrs. Ygorre smiled faintly. "Sorry. Ygorres don't kiss and tell."

"But people are going into comas," said Benny. "Please?"

She wiped her mouth, dropped her napkin onto her plate, and shook her head. "Professional ethics. We break the code of silence, and next thing you know, it's all villagers with torches storming the castle."

"But the haunting—" I said.

"Is definitely *not* the work of my former employer," said Mrs. Ygorre. "He has no interest in ghosts." She stood. "Esme, would you show your friends out? I have a Skype interview to prepare for."

She politely shook hands with us and made her exit.

Esme sighed, laying aside her sketch pad. "You're *so* not my friends."

"Don't worry, sunshine," said Benny. "Nobody's putting you on BFF speed dial."

But as she hustled us out of the house, I couldn't help feeling a stab of sympathy for Miss Mini-Goth. Couldn't be much of a home life, moving from place to place while your mom did creepy work for a variety of nutjobs.

"See you in school," I said to Esme at the door.

"Sure thing," she said. "Unless some creature of the night paralyzes you and sucks out your innards like a meat milk shake."

And on that cheery note, we left.

Chapter Thirteen

All Stings Considered

ON OUR RIDE BACK to school that evening, worries churned through my brain like hammerheads in a shark tank. Could Benny and I identify the haunting's source without falling victim to it? Could Mrs. Ygorre's mysterious employer be behind all the monsters that had been showing up recently in Monterrosa? Were my parents really fine, like Abuelita said, or were they teetering on the edge of divorce?

And would Hollywood ever make an Incredible Hulk movie that didn't stink like a vulture's lunch box? (This one had been bothering me for years.)

The sun was dipping over the horizon as we parked our bikes outside the mechanical room.

"Perfect," said Benny. "We've got an hour to spend here before we have to be home for dinner."

"Good thing," I said. "We're having chile rellenos tonight; I'd hate to miss it."

Our conversation stayed light, but I could tell from his tone that Benny was as tense as I was. We unlocked the door and flipped on the light. After carefully surveying as much of the room as we could see from the threshold, we went inside.

"First things first," said Benny. "Hold up your phone and show the time."

I obeyed, while Benny angled his phone to take a selfie of us in the room.

"There's Tyler's proof," he said. "Now for our equipment."

"Equipment?"

Unzipping his book bag, Benny laid out a series of items on the cold concrete floor: two black-light flashlights, a half-dozen candles, a wooden cross, a plate, some rope, a fistful of gluten-free quinoa cookies (don't ask), three apples, a Snickers bar, and two colas.

"Planning to spend the night?" I said.

Benny cleared his throat. "A Boy Scout is always prepared."

"You're not a Boy Scout."

He whipped off a quick salute. "And I never let that stop me. I figure we set up the candles and offering, just like Miss Freshley did, turn off the overhead lights, and use these cool black-light rigs to spot the ghost."

Benny held a flashlight under his chin, for that jack-o'-lantern look.

"It's the real you," I said.

"They'll help us see ghosts that are invisible to others."

Together, we laid the food on the plate, stood the candles in a circle, and lit them. When Benny turned off the lights, I don't mind telling you the place was more than a little spooky.

I missed the comfort of Mrs. T's presence.

"Let's give it a while and see what happens," said Benny.

We stood in the center of the circle, clutching our flashlights and peering around us. Time stretched. One of the boilers ticked. Benny fidgeted. The longer we stood there with nothing happening, the tighter my shoulders got.

Benny gave a nervous chuckle and reached for a soda. "Think the ghost would mind if I took a little sip?"

"It's supposed to be an offering," I said.

"Yeah, but ghosts don't have throats, and mine is parched." After a quick check around, he popped the top on a can and slurped some down, snagging the Snickers for good measure.

That's Benny all over—ready to risk supernatural wrath for a snack.

We waited for about forty-five minutes, until the suspense had me ready to peel off my own skin. I switched on my flashlight.

"That's it, I'm taking a look around," I said.

"Lead on," said Benny, sticking close.

Leaving the circle, we began to explore the mechanical room. The massive boilers and other machines loomed above us like glowering giants, while the ducts and pipes snaked away in all directions.

No ghosts raised their heads; no supernatural beasties attacked us. Could the haunting have ended on its own?

"Hey, check this out," said Benny, shining the flashlight on his face. "Who's got the whitest teeth in fourth grade?"

His choppers glowed in the ultraviolet light like a mouthful of fireflies.

"I guess that sandpaper toothbrush really paid off," I said, relaxing a little. And of course, just when I started to relax . . .

Scritch scritch-scritch.

Something scuttled behind one of the boilers. I swung my flashlight that way and caught a glimpse of glowing blue-green.

"What the—?" My knees trembled.

Rigid as steel underpants, Benny and I followed the phantom with flashlights held out like swords. Slowly, carefully, we peeked around the huge metal drum and came face-to-face with our ghost.

But of course, it wasn't a ghost. It was a hissing freak of nature.

"Whoa!" cried Benny.

"That's just . . . wrong," I said.

About the size of a jumbo pit bull, the creature was part lion, part scorpion, and entirely spooky. Its fangs dripped, its pincers clacked. The creature's armored back plates glowed in the black light like a swimming pool at night. Its scorpion tail swayed like an angry cobra.

This thing meant business.

"Gaah!" I stumbled back, bumped into a pipe, and something behind me hissed.

And that's when I learned that the creature had a mate.

Four feet away.

Whose tail was already in motion.

"*¡Hijole!*" My feet felt as heavy as cinder blocks. I tried to move, but—

Down whipped the stinger, piercing my outflung hand.

"Aah!" I cried.

Benny rushed forward, shining his flashlight in the monster's eyes and stomping his feet. "Yah! Get out of here!" he yelled at it.

Amazingly, it worked. The creature scuttled backward on its cat paws, leaving us enough room to dash for the exit.

My hand throbbed, radiating pain. My legs were heavy and clumsy. I staggered after Benny, and the journey back to our candlelit circle seemed to last longer than Christopher Columbus's voyage.

Noticing I'd fallen behind, Benny came back for me. "Are you hurt?" he said. "Where'd it get you?"

"The . . . hand," I mumbled. My tongue felt as thick as a chorizo sausage.

"Lean on me." Benny guided me to the circle.

Fire raced along my veins. My skin radiated heat; even my eyeballs sizzled. Nightmare images flashed through my mind, one after the other, unstoppable.

All my classmates in a coma, lying side by side in the hospital.

Being banned from school for my failures.

The Amazing Spider-Man comic book, canceled forever.

"Horrible," I muttered, gripping Benny's shirt. "So horrible."

"What is?" said Benny. His voice seemed to come all the way from Connecticut in a tin box.

But I couldn't find words. The images kept rolling like a runaway horror movie, seeming more real than the room around me.

My dad losing his job, my sister crying, my parents getting divorced.

Me leaving Monterrosa for good.

A mean voice in my head said, *You're responsible. This is all your fault.*

"No!" I cried. "I tried to stop them, but they wouldn't listen!"

Benny paused just inside our candle circle. He lifted my hand.

"Uh-oh," he said. "That thing looks infected."

I tried to see what he was talking about, but my eyes wouldn't obey me. Naughty eyes, I thought, fuzzily. Send 'em to the corner without any supper.

"I'm gonna sterilize it," said Benny. He reached down and plucked something from the offering plate.

"All my fault," I mumbled. "Couldn't keep them together."

Despair sapped my strength. My eyes wanted to roll back in my head. I fought the urge. I wasn't ready to spend my life in a coma.

And still the visions came. I saw my mom and Veronica moving out of our house, and the weight of sadness nearly crushed me. At the same time, in real life, I saw Benny raising the cola can. Some part of my mind said, Silly Benny—can't sterilize with soda.

"Hold still." He poured the fizzy liquid onto my wound.

It was like dipping my hand in lava.

I screamed. The pain swelled, ten times worse than the sting itself. Gripping my wrist, I jackknifed in two.

"¡Dios mío! Wha . . . ?" I choked out.

"Choose cola, choose life," said Benny. "I figured if it can strip rust off of nails, it might help with the poison."

Oddly enough, he seemed to be onto something. Defeated by the all-consuming agony in my hand, the tide of visions ebbed. My eyes obeyed me again, the fever in my blood cooled.

"Give me that!" I snapped.

Snatching the soda, I poured half of what remained over my wounded hand and chugged the rest.

As though I had flipped a switch, the pain faded almost entirely. I was myself again.

"Are you okay?" said Benny.

I slugged his upper arm with my uninjured hand. "That hurt!" I said. "And thanks for saving me."

Rubbing his shoulder, Benny said, "You're welcome. Um, where are the lorpions?"

"Lorp—?" I'd been so consumed by pain, I'd forgotten about the creature that stung me.

We flashed our beams around the room and picked out the two monsters about fifteen feet away, crouched and waiting. Then my skin prickled as two more scorpion-lions (lorpions? sclions?) stalked forward from the shadows to join them.

I tensed. "You know that the candles won't stop them, right?"

"Duh," said Benny. "Keep your flashlight on them. I just need to do one thing. . . ." He brought up his phone and snapped a photo, saying, "Cheese!"

Rrruaaghh! The monsters roared in chorus, startled by the flash.

That was enough for us. Benny and I beat feet out of there like the Terminator himself was on our heels.

Chapter Fourteen

Manilow
Overboard

THE BIKE RIDE HOME was like watching a zombie movie in Swahili—confusing, scary, and full of unanswered questions. Plus, my limbs were still wobbly after my sting, so we had to flee slowly.

"Well, the good news is, we don't have ghosts," I said. My voice wobbled a bit.

Benny gave a shaky laugh. "And we know what made those big paw prints Mr. Boo showed us."

"Yay, us."

We rolled along in silence for a while, still trying to deal with what we'd seen.

"A scorpion mixed with a lion?" said Benny. "How is that even possible?"

"I know." My heart thudded faster at the thought of the creatures. Benny and I pedaled onward, through pools of light cast by streetlamps.

"I've got a C in science, and even *I* know that insects can't breed with mammals," he said. "Plus, there's the whole size difference."

I shook my head. Traces of my poison-caused visions still shadowed me. Melancholy made me sluggish.

"Poor José," I murmured. "Poor Mr. Boo and the rest."

"The victims?"

I nodded. "First, they get blasted with images of their worst fears, then they fall into a permanent sleep."

Benny glanced over at me. "That's what happened to you? Hallucinations?"

I tried to swallow around a lump in my throat that felt like an ostrich egg. "It was awful. And if you hadn't been there, I'd be in a coma right now."

Benny's smirk was wistful. "Remember that, come Christmastime. Only sixteen more shopping days left."

"Seriously," I said. "You saved me. That was quick thinking."

He sat up a little straighter. "It was, wasn't it? Pure instinct, you know. Maybe I'll become a doctor."

"But first, Dr. Brackman, we've got to tell the hospital how soda counteracts the poison."

"Absolutely," said Benny. "We'll just call them up, and, uh . . ." He petered out as a thought hit him.

I sagged in my seat, having the same realization. "And tell them, 'Hey, just pour soda over your comatose patients. That'll save 'em. No, really, it will.'"

Benny rubbed his jaw. "Yeah, we might need to work on the wording."

As our bikes leaned into a curve, I said, "We'll get on it tonight. But right now there's another problem on my mind."

"How high to make the monument to my awesomeness?" said Benny.

I sent him a sober look. "How the heck do we drive those monsters out of town?"

He had no answer for that one.

Turning off the main road, we entered our neighborhood. Blue TV-screen light shone from living room windows. The burble of dinnertime conversation drifted into the night. These people were relaxed, happy. They had no clue about what lurked in our school.

"You know, Mrs. Johnson would want us to tell her about this," I said.

"Yeah," said Benny.

"And then back off," I said.

"Yeah," he repeated.

I shifted on my seat. "Somehow, that doesn't sound very heroic."

"Nope," Benny agreed, "it doesn't."

I didn't know why (stubbornness? revenge?) but I didn't

want to just step away from this problem. Not yet. I wanted us to come up with a solution on our own.

"We've got a day and a half," I said as we turned into my driveway. "How about we try a couple of things tomorrow, and if they don't work, *then* we tell the principal?"

Benny's grin was as wide as the waistband of a hippo's tutu. "See? I knew my positive influence would rub off on you."

We parked our bikes by my garage and headed inside. Tomorrow we'd tackle the monster problem. But tonight? The first thing I did was give my dad and Abuelita a great big hug.

The next morning, before school, we lugged my sister's karaoke machine to the mechanical room. Our reasoning was, since the scorpion-lions were part cat (okay, lion), maybe we could drive them out with stuff that cats hate. Near the top of that list, Benny assured me, was loud music.

When we reached the room, I'm not ashamed to say I let Benny go inside first. The thought of those scorpion tails still gave me the cold shivers.

"The coast is clear," Benny said. "Let's blast out some lorpions."

I grimaced. "Still don't think that name is working."

"What do you want us to call them, then?" he said. "Sclions?"

I cocked my head. "Almost. How about . . . scorp-lions?"

"Scorp-lions . . ." Benny tried it out and nodded. "Scorp-lions it is."

That settled, we plugged in the unit, angling it to give the room maximum coverage. The night before, I had gone through my sister's karaoke CDs to find the most annoying one.

Reaching into my book bag, I dug out the disc I borrowed from her collection.

Benny squinted at it. "Who's . . . Barry Manilow?"

"A scorp-lion's worst nightmare," I said, slipping the CD into the player. "Crank it up."

As soon as the soppy strings and drippy vocals blasted from the speakers, Benny winced. "Ugh, this is putrid!" he shouted.

"Perfect!" I yelled.

We retreated outside before the music made our ears bleed.

"I can't believe anyone would want to sing this stuff," said Benny.

"That's my sister for you," I said, watching the half-open door. "Too bad she isn't here to sing now. Those scorp-lions wouldn't know what hit them."

A few minutes passed. The second song was even worse than the first. But the monsters didn't show.

"Anytime now," said Benny.

We waited. And waited. I actually started humming along with one of the songs before Benny stopped me. Two more tunes went by. Incoming students gave us strange looks as they passed down the hall.

But still no scorp-lions.

Something occurred to me. "Hey, Benny."

"Yeah?"

"Did we put the speakers in the wrong place?"

He frowned. "What do you mean?"

"We're trying to drive the monsters *out*, but the music is loudest right by the door. Wouldn't they head in the other direction?"

"Good point," said Benny, slumping. Then his face brightened. "Hey, I just realized something."

"That you'll never beat me in *Minecraft*?"

He flashed me a fake smile. "Ha-ha. No, that there must be some kind of tunnel between this room and the portables. How else would these guys be able to sting people in both places and not be seen?"

"Makes sense. So they've probably retreated into their tunnel." I looked him up and down. "You know, you're a lot brighter than they say."

Benny held a finger to his lips. "*Shhh*. If word gets around, Mr. Chu will expect a lot more of me."

I scratched my head. "So how do we drive the monsters out completely? Blast music at both ends?"

"Nope," said Benny, patting his book bag. "We take it to the next level."

But before I could learn what the next level was, the bell rang. Time to pack up the karaoke system and hustle off to Mr. Chu's room. Maybe, if I got him to sing a few tunes, he'd never find out I didn't have time to do the math homework last night.

I sighed.

Being a hero and a student at the same time is a lot harder than it looks.

Chapter Fifteen

The Big Stink

THERE WAS NO SINGING in class. Instead, we worked on our Greek helmets and shields, which were almost finished. But all I could think was, There's a ticking time bomb under the school, and we've got to defuse it. And quickly, before any more victims fall into comas.

When the recess bell rang, Benny and I launched out the door like pebbles from a slingshot. As we trotted down the hall, Benny patted his book bag.

"Wait till you get a load of this," he crowed. "It's awesome."

"Can't wait."

Once again, we slipped through the door into the mechanical room. Benny and I were spending so much time there it was starting to feel like a home away from home. Maybe I'd decorate it with some comfy throw pillows and an Xbox station—as soon as we got rid of the monsters.

"Okay, so what's our Plan B?" I asked.

Benny dipped into his backpack and set several baggies on the floor with a flourish. "Ta-da!"

"We're going to drive them off with leftovers?" I asked. "I mean, I know your mom's tofu nut loaf is pretty scary, but—"

"This," he said, raising one of the bags to eye level, "nearly got my brother suspended in eighth grade."

I eyeballed it. There was a smaller bag inside the baggie. The inner one held liquid, and the outer one some kind of powder.

"Okay, so what is it?" I asked.

Benny's grin dripped with devilment. "The most powerful stink bomb known to mankind—or at least, student-kind."

"Cool!" I took it from him and examined the thing. "How does it work?"

"Squeeze the inner bag till it pops, then run like heck." He cackled.

"I meant, how does it make the stink?"

Benny shrugged, impatient. "I dunno. It's chemistry."

Carefully, I handed the stink bomb back to him. "And it'll do the trick?"

"Cats hate strong smells. This'll have the scorp-lions out of their burrow and running for the hills in no time."

"Then, bombs away!" I said.

We set the bags in a line near the most likely tunnel location. I wasn't about to risk another sting by poking around for the actual mouth of the passage. Then . . .

"Careful not to pop the outside bag," said Benny, "or we'll get gassed."

With all the care of a newbie brain surgeon, we gently squeezed until we burst the four inner bags.

"Now haul buns!" cried Benny.

World Cup soccer players wished they had the kind of speed Benny and I turned on that day. In a mad rush, we blasted across the room and out the door, slamming and locking it behind us.

"Now what?" I said.

"We take a well-deserved play break, and let science do its work."

Fifteen minutes later, we were back in class, just settling in. I wondered how our latest attempt was working. Had the scorp-lions run off? And how would we know when they had? Mr. Chu let us work on our science-fair projects while he strolled around the room, checking our progress.

"Blinding them with science?" he asked Tina.

"Hopefully not," she said. "It's . . . a song reference."

She pursed her lips and got back to work.

Tina was demonstrating self-inflating balloons. Tyler and Pete's project concerned paper-airplane aerodynamics.

I assumed Esme Ygorre would try to animate a corpse, like Dr. Frankenstein.

And then it struck me.

"We have no project," I told Benny.

He scowled. "You're right. How did we miss that?"

"Maybe because we've been spending all our time trying to get rid of monsters?"

"Maybe." Benny brightened, snapping his fingers. "Hey, that could be our project!"

My forehead crinkled. "The scientific way to get rid of monsters?"

"Exactly!" He held up a hand modestly. "It's okay. You don't need to say it—I'm brilliant."

"That's good, 'cause I wasn't going to say it."

Unfortunately, I didn't have any better ideas, so we set to work writing it up. But before Mr. Chu could check on us, our project announced itself to the class.

"Eew," said Hannah. "What's that smell?"

"Whoever smelt it, dealt it!" cried Big Pete, with a chortle. I don't know why, but someone's always got to make this comment.

I sniffed but didn't notice anything beyond a very faint egg-y odor.

Still, I could track the stench rolling like a wave from the far wall, just by monitoring my classmates' reactions.

"OMG!" squealed Cheyenne.

"Ugh!" grunted Tyler.

"Gross!" said Gabi.

Kids fanned the air, held their noses, or hid their faces.

And then the wave reached Benny and me. I nearly gagged on the stink.

It was rotten eggs, mixed with spoiled meat, mixed with the nastiest public toilet you've ever encountered. If smells were movie monsters, this was the King Kong champion of stenchiness.

"Pee-yew!" I moaned. "What's in that stuff?"

"Chemicals," said Benny. His smile showed behind the hand he'd clapped over his nose. "Isn't science great?"

"Okay, did someone choose stink-bomb construction for their science project?" asked Mr. Chu. "If so, please dial it down."

Benny and I carefully kept a straight face. Just our luck—a psychic teacher.

"Tyler?" said Mr. Chu. "Was it you?"

"Wasn't me," Tyler gasped. "Why don't you ask Benny and Carlos?"

"Yeah," said AJ, with a glare. "They're up to lots of suspicious stuff." And this coming from the kid we rescued from mutant mantises two weeks earlier. Where's the gratitude?

Our teacher turned my way. "How about it, Carlos?"

"I promise you," said Benny before I could speak, "we

would never choose something as gross as stink bombs for our project."

And that was true—technically speaking.

As they spoke, the smell thickened, then thickened again, like a killer fog in a horror movie. My eyes were actually watering.

Jackson said, "I think—ugh—it's coming from the heater vents."

Amrita raised her hand. "Permission to toss my cookies?" she asked Mr. Chu.

"Okay, that's it!" he cried. "Time to abandon ship. Everyone, form a line now."

You'd have thought they were handing out free As at the door, our class lined up so fast. We trotted down the hallway and out onto the grass, joining what looked like every other classroom in the school.

"Those things are strong," I muttered to Benny.

"Like I said—strongest known to man," he replied.

Outside, the air was cool and fresh—and more importantly, stench-free. I gulped it gratefully.

Benny nudged me. "If that doesn't drive 'em out, I don't know what will."

At that, an unhappy thought struck me. "But if we do drive them out . . ."

"Yeah?" said Benny.

"Where will they go next? They could be anywhere."

I glanced around, chills crawling up my shoulders. "The playground, the park, the cafeteria . . ."

"Don't worry," said Benny. "They love dark, underground places, right?"

"Right."

"So they must have gotten here through tunnels, and they'll probably leave the same way."

I cocked my head, not totally convinced. "Maybe, but—"

Just then, Tyler Spork swaggered down the line to us, trailed by Big Pete. "So, losers, ready to admit you're totally chicken?"

"What are you talking about?" I asked, still eyeing the bushes for monsters.

Tyler shared a smirk with Pete. "Last night," he said. "No way did you guys spend an hour in there with the ghost."

Benny handed him an answering smirk and fished out his phone. Displaying the first photo from the night before, he said, "Watch it and weep, sucka!"

Frowning, Tyler and Pete checked out our mechanical room selfie.

"That doesn't prove anything," Pete said. "You could've shot it and left."

"Oh, yeah?" Benny advanced to the scorp-lion photo. "Then how do you explain . . . this?"

But before he could show them, a shadow fell over us. "And just what," said Principal Johnson, "do we have here?"

Chapter Sixteen

Mixed Troubles

I KNEW WE'D DONE nothing wrong—well, almost nothing. (It was for the highest good, after all.) But my heart still climbed into my throat when Mrs. Johnson pulled Benny and me out of line for a private conversation.

"Well?" she said. "You've been investigating this . . . situation for a full day. What do you have to report?"

I offered up a sickly smile. "Um, there's good news and bad news."

"Isn't there always?" Her eyebrow arched. "Go on."

"The good news is, we found what was putting people into comas," I said.

"And the bad?" asked Mrs. Johnson.

Benny showed her the photo. "This. Their sting knocks people out."

"That's the best you can do?" she said. "Photoshopped monsters?"

"It's not Photoshopped," said Benny.

"He's telling the truth," I added. "We don't even know how to use the program."

"No kidding?" Our principal grimaced at the image. "Then what in the *Wide World of Sports* is that?"

"We call them scorp-lions," said Benny.

"That's awful!" she said.

I jammed my hands into my pockets. "Well, it was the best name we could think of."

Mrs. Johnson cut her eyes at me. "Not the name, the creature."

"Oh."

Her gaze flicked down at the photo, then up at the restless students all around us. "I should close down the school right now," she said. "All these kids. The danger . . ."

"Well, sure," said Benny. "You could shut things down, but we may have just taken care of the problem."

"Explain yourself," said Mrs. Johnson.

Benny's chest swelled. "We left something in the mechanical room that the scorp-lions really hate. In fact, I bet they're already running away on their furry little feet."

She stared at him for a moment, and then her eyes widened. "That was you two? That nasty smell?"

"Um . . ." I said. Suddenly the air around us felt frostier than an igloo with a moonroof.

"Well," said Benny, oblivious. "I don't like to brag, but—"

"You disrupted classes throughout this school and drove everyone from their rooms?" The principal's eyes narrowed like a gunslinger's at high noon. "Not knowing if those creatures would be roaming around outside?"

"Uh, yeah?" said Benny. He seemed less certain.

"*And* you deliberately ignored my instructions by trying to deal with things yourself instead of calling me?"

I jumped in. "Technically yes, but we—"

Mrs. Johnson's expression looked meaner than a mama wasp. "I should lock you up in detention and throw away the key."

"But you said we'd each get two free passes," Benny protested.

Her nostrils flared. "Consider this your first one."

"Yes, ma'am," I said. "Thank you, ma'am."

Principal Johnson planted her fists on her hips, looked up at the sky, and blew out some air. "I'd just as soon bite a bug as work with you two again."

"Thanks," said Benny. "We try."

"That wasn't a compliment." She took a moment to collect herself. "Now, I'll say this in a way that not even you can misinterpret, Mr. Brackman."

I grimaced. When principals call you Mister, it's never a good sign.

"First," said Mrs. Johnson, "text me that photo so I can send it to Pest Control. And second: Stay. Out. Of. That. Room. *¿Comprende?*"

"Yes, ma'am," we said together.

"But we can still take a quick peek inside, right?" said Benny. "Just to be sure they've gone?"

The principal's gaze was a slow burn. "Not a peek, not a sniff, not a glimmer. And just to make sure . . ."

"Yes?" I asked.

"Key, please."

With a wistful look, Benny handed her the universal key. She made a shooing gesture with both hands. "Now git! Go join your class."

You can always tell when Mrs. Johnson is upset—her Texas twang gets strong enough to raise a blood blister on a boot. When that happens, the smart move is to follow orders. We're not that smart, but still, we went and joined our class.

"Geez," said Benny. "Would it have killed her to say thanks?"

Like the other teachers, Mr. Chu ended up conducting our lessons on the playground until jumbo-sized electric fans could air out the classrooms. Amrita and Cheyenne complained bitterly about not being able to work on their science-fair projects. But I didn't mind.

Hopefully, our project was taking care of itself right that moment. With a little luck, the monsters had fled back into whatever underground tunnels they'd come from, and all that remained was to learn the chemical content of Benny's stink bombs for our write-up. Easy-peasy, sweet and greasy.

When the all-clear bell rang, everyone fell into lines and trudged back to class.

"Hey," Benny said as we walked down the hall, "how do we tell if the you-know-whats are gone, if we can't go check out the room?"

I lifted a shoulder. "Nobody else gets stung, and the moaning stops?"

"Works for me."

Tina pulled up beside us. "So what did the principal want?"

"To congratulate us on our excellent grades," said Benny.

She snorted. "In your dreams, Brackman. What did she really want?"

"We're doing a little project for her," I said.

"You mean busting up the haunting?" said Tina.

My mouth fell open. "How did you know?"

One corner of her mouth tugged upward. "That's your only talent, aside from buying comic books and making wisecracks."

She laughed at my expression. "Nah, Tyler's been blabbing about his dare, and I connected the dots. So, what's the latest on our spook situation?"

We gave her the lowdown, and before we'd finished, discovered that we had an eavesdropper: Esme. Benny noticed her first.

"How much did you hear, Nosy McSnoopersteen?" he asked.

Tossing back her long black hair, Esme said, "You've got a monster problem and you're in way over your head. Just as I predicted."

"Predicted?" I said. "You told everyone it was a ghost."

Esme flapped her hand. "Ghost, monster, whatever. Shout when you need my expert help."

"Don't you worry." Benny's grin oozed smugness. "The real experts have already handled it."

But then, only ten minutes after we'd settled back into our lessons, that creepy moaning echoed once again through the vents. The "real experts" hadn't handled anything. Those scorp-lions were dug in deeper than a deer tick in a hound dog's ear.

I met Benny's exasperated gaze. We both knew what this meant. Come lunchtime, we'd have to work on Plan C.

And we didn't have a Plan C. Fact is, we were running out of both plans and resourcefulness. And the clock was ticking.

Chapter Seventeen

The Next
Pest Thing

AS WE LEFT the lunchroom after a hurried meal, Benny and I came across an argument in the hall. Not so strange, maybe. Kids get into beefs every day. But this time, it was Principal Johnson and two guys in tan overalls mixing it up.

"You said you had scorpions," said the first man, whose potbelly was so big he seemed to be smuggling a basketball under his outfit.

"I do," said Mrs. Johnson, her voice flatter than month-old roadkill.

"Those ain't scorpions," whined the second guy, a short dude with forearms like Thor. "They're f-freaks of nature." The whites of his eyes showed all around. The man was clearly spooked.

"Keep your voice down." Our principal crossed her arms. "Either way, they're pests. You say you get rid of pests."

Basketball Belly scoffed. "Sure, little bitty ones."

"Are you big, tough hombres afraid of varmints?" she said.

"We're not afraid of anything," the potbellied man growled.

"Doesn't look like it to me."

Shorty held up his palms. "Lady, we handle bedbugs, spiders, rats, roaches, and termites. I ain't never tackled anything big enough to eat my poodle. Did you see that thing?"

Glancing around for eavesdroppers, she shushed the pest guy.

"Did you see it?" he repeated, in a hoarse whisper. "That's way out of our league."

"You're saying you won't even try?" Icicles formed on Mrs. Johnson's words.

"We're saying this is a job for Animal Control," said Basketball Belly, hoisting his sprayer onto his shoulder. "Why don't you give them a call?"

"Oh, I will," she said. "And don't expect a positive review on Yelp."

After exchanging a final round of glares, the men collected their equipment and slouched off down the hall. Mrs. Johnson wheeled on us.

"Don't even dream of sticking your noses into it," she said.

"Who, us?" said Benny, with his best Little Angel expression.

"Animal Control will handle this."

"Of course," I said. "But if anyone gets stung, tell them to pour soda over the wound. It stops the coma."

Mrs. Johnson sent me a dubious look, which was about the same response the hospital had given us when we called with that same message. Then she sniffed, spun on her heel, and headed for the office.

"Think Animal Control can handle it?" I asked Benny.

He grunted. "Yeah, right."

As we paced the playground brainstorming Plan C, I spotted Esme sitting on a low wall by the basketball courts. A thought struck me. "Maybe there's another way to approach this."

"How do you mean?" asked Benny.

"We've been treating the monsters like cats, and it hasn't helped."

"True," said Benny. "So now we treat 'em like scorpions and break out the bug spray?"

"Not exactly. I think if we knew more about them, we could try a different approach—something that works."

Benny brightened. "I'm all ears," he said. "Except for the parts of me that are eyes, nose, neck, and so forth."

I pointed at Miss Mini-Goth. "Maybe she's got the key."

"Esme?" he said. "Off-key, maybe."

"Just follow my lead." I strolled over and sat beside her on the wall. Benny took her other side.

"How's it going?" I said.

Esme glanced at me sidelong. "You need my help. The big bad monster experts need my help."

I sighed. "Much as I hate to admit it. Benny, show her the picture."

He pulled out his phone and scrolled to the scorp-lion photo.

"This is what we're dealing with," I said.

Esme's face softened. "Aww, cute! Look at their little tails."

Benny and I traded a look over her head. "Uh, yeah," I said. "We're wondering whether these . . . cuties might have been created by your mom's old boss?"

She squinted at the image, then wagged her head "Mmm, maybe. Whoever it was did a good job. It's not easy splicing insects and mammals."

"Like mixing peanut butter and garlic," said Benny.

"Uh, yeah, but only a million times harder," said Esme, with an eye roll. "I bet the DNA isn't even compatible, and—"

"Fascinating," I said. "And we'd love to talk to your mom's old boss about it."

She shrugged. "I don't know his name. Mom had to sign some agreement that she couldn't discuss her job, even with me."

I sagged. So much for that bright idea.

"Bummer," said Benny. He made to stand. "Well, we—"

"Hang on," I said to Esme, grasping at straws. "You must know *something* about him. A clue to where he lives? Anything?"

Esme caught a strand of her hair between her lips and chewed it thoughtfully. "Well," she said after a pause, "he's really rich."

"Go on," I said.

"When my mom worked for him, a long black limo took her to and from work every day. And I think it's somewhere in Monterrosa."

"That narrows it down," said Benny. "Barely."

Esme's gaze tracked the basketball players as she continued to gnaw on her hair. "Oh, and he's old, I think, and he might be from another country."

"Why do you say that?" I asked.

"When things got really bad between them, she once said, 'I wish that chuckleheaded old poop would go back where he came from.' That's all I can remember."

Chuckleheaded old poop? An idea itched at the back of my mind.

Standing, I said, "Thanks, that's a big help."

"It is?" said Esme. "Then do me a favor."

"What's that?" asked Benny.

A smile drifted across her pale face like a wispy cloud. "Introduce me to that redheaded guy playing basketball."

"Why?" I asked.

"He's dreamy." Esme's heavily mascaraed eyelashes fluttered like a pair of dirty moths trying to take flight.

I grimaced. "Eew!"

"What?" said Esme. "He's cute!"

"Eeeww!" cried Benny and I together. As we hustled off before the cooties could catch us, I called back to her, "Connor's a fifth grader, anyway."

"Connor," she breathed.

Pausing in a quiet corner of the playground, I told Benny, "See? We really learned something there."

"That girls are nothing but googly-eyed cootie magnets?" he said.

"Besides that," I said. "She said the monster-making guy was old, rich, and not from around here. Who do we know like that?"

Benny frowned. "Arnold Schwarzenegger?"

"In Monterrosa," I said.

Cocking his head, Benny said, "Well, there's Mr. Chen, who owns all those supermarkets."

"Yeah, but he's *real* old," I said. "I can't see him making anything stronger than tea. Ooh, what about Mr. Papadakis?"

"The finance guy? I heard he was so afraid of trick-or-treaters he locked his front gate and hid behind the curtains."

I rubbed my jaw. "Hmm . . ."

Then, in a flash, the answer hit us both.

"The science dude," said Benny.

"Hanzomon," I said. "The guy who wanted new heroes."

A strange expression crossed Benny's face. He placed his fingers on his temples and shut his eyes.

"What's wrong?" I asked. "Headache?"

"I . . . I'm having a psychic moment."

"You can see the future?" Had he caught ESP from Miss Freshley? I wondered.

"My vision is clearing. I see . . . I see Mr. Hanzomon's office getting a couple of late-night visitors."

I smirked. "You're some psychic, all right. The Great Benzini strikes again."

Chapter Eighteen

Three Dog Fright

OUR PLAN, like most plans Benny and I hatched, was a simple one. (Rocket scientists we weren't.) Step One: learn where Mr. Hanzomon worked. Step Two: slip out at night and go visit his office. Step Three: snoop around until we learned something about the monsters.

Steps One and Two were simple enough. When we said we wanted to write the scientist a thank-you letter for the iPads, Mrs. Johnson shared his business address.

"Glad to see you're not trying to convince me to let you into the mechanical room," said the principal.

"We've learned our lesson," said Benny.

We hadn't really. All we'd learned was to be sneakier.

And we put our sneakiness to good use that night. After

my dad had gone to bed, I crept into the kitchen to collect some helpful supplies. I was loading up my book bag when I heard the telltale clickety-click of doggie toenails.

Zeppo padded up to me. He wagged, giving me the Bambi eyes. Once a moocher, always a moocher.

"Go away," I whispered. "Shoo!"

But he just sat there, tongue hanging out. Zeppo the chowhound was convinced that anytime someone entered the kitchen, it was to feed him. As I shut my bag, he began to whine.

"Shhh!" I checked the hallway door. The last thing I needed was to wake up my dad. "All right, all right. You win."

Opening the fridge, I scrounged up some leftover chicken and dropped a chunk to the floor. Zeppo pounced on it like Spider-Man on Doc Ock. Hmm . . . that gave me an idea. I popped some hamburger into my bag, just in case the Hanzomon offices had a watchdog, then I tossed another chicken morsel to Zeppo. While he was occupied, I tiptoed back to my room and slipped out the window.

Benny was waiting in the field between our two houses. Our bikes stood beside him. "You're late," he whispered.

"Doggie blackmail," I said. "Let's go."

Like a big fat graffiti artist, the moon had painted the trees and bushes with silver. As we threaded our bikes down the trail, TV noises still rose from our neighbors' houses, so we kept our traps shut. An image of my dad sleeping entered my head. Was he dreaming of my mom? Or dreaming of life without her? I shivered.

When Benny and I reached the street, I pushed the vision away. Time to focus. We mounted up and pedaled down the street.

"Hey, what if this Hanzomon guy has guard dogs?" said Benny.

"Thought of that." I patted my book bag. Then my face fell. "But what if he has actual guard-guards?"

Benny's smile flashed milky white in the moonlight. "I brought a distraction." He waggled his eyebrows. "You know, between the two of us, we're actually kind of smart."

"Then how come we've gotten into so much trouble?"

Benny pursed his lips. "I did say 'kind of.'"

We pedaled on in silence for a while. Past the empty Little League field, past the construction site, skirting areas where people might spot us. Before long, we reached Via Madrugada, which wound through the low hills just outside of town. Rich-people territory.

When the road turned steep, we walked our bikes, stopping at last in front of some fancy wrought-iron gates, right out of a Dracula movie.

Benny checked the address. "Here we are," he said. "Office, sweet office."

I took in the ivy-covered wall, the security lights, the nearly empty parking lot, and the electronic gizmo that controlled the gate. My muscles felt twitchy. Suddenly this didn't seem like such a hot idea.

"How will we even get inside?" I whispered. "It's probably locked up tighter than Fort Knox."

Benny waved off my worry. "We'll find a way in. They always do in the movies."

"Yeah; but, Benny?"

"What?"

"This isn't the movies," I said.

Nevertheless, we'd already come all the way out there. Might as well give it a try. We stashed our bikes along the side of the wall and checked the street for witnesses.

All clear. The neighborhood was as quiet as a puma hiding in the long grass.

Despite my sudden conviction that this was a very bad plan, I followed as Benny began scaling the thick ivy stalks. Up we climbed, until we swung our legs over and sat astride the wall. I was relieved to find no barbed wire or broken glass up there.

For some reason, this billionaire wasn't all that worried about security. I didn't know whether or not I should be worried about that.

"Check it out," Benny whispered.

Behind the walls sprawled a massive three-story structure. It looked like a Spanish castle and a Ukrainian embassy had had a baby, then buried it in bling. The place was all golden gargoyles and turrets, onion domes and red-tiled roof—just a wee bit unusual for an office. Up top, a spotlight illuminated the blue Hanzomon International sign. The lower two stories were dark; lights showed in only three top-floor windows.

"Perfect," said Benny.

"Sure," I said. "If you're a billionaire with more money than taste."

The ivy grew more sparsely on the inside wall, but it was thick enough. Benny began his descent. And, with a sinking feeling in my gut like the one you get just before the roller coaster plummets, I followed.

Paving stones traced a dimly lit path between bushes shaped into wolves and mastodons and freakier hedge animals. As usual, Benny plunged ahead while I brought up the rear. When the pathway forked, we took the turning that seemed to lead toward the back of the building.

"So far, so good," Benny whispered.

But I wasn't so sure. This kind of garden might have *real* animals in it.

My busy imagination supplied tigers, Dobermans, and hungry Komodo dragons lurking around each corner. Also visions of my dad's disgust and disappointment when he came to identify my remains. Sneaking out of the house was one thing. Sneaking out and getting eaten while trespassing was a whole other ball game.

So when something rustled in the bushes to our left, I nearly leaped out of my skin. "What was that?"

We froze. The moon ducked behind a cloud, and the dim garden lights revealed nothing.

"Probably just a possum," whispered Benny after a tense pause. "Come on."

More slowly now, we crept along the path. When we were almost even with the office building, the rustling came again.

"Possums are shy," I whispered.

"Yeah, so?"

"So why is this possum following us?"

His reassuring grin looked a bit frayed around the edges. "It's, uh, lonely?"

Just twenty steps more to the nearest side door. For me, those steps couldn't come fast enough. "Hurry," I whispered.

The path curved around one last, shaggy bush. And when we reached the other side, we met the possum.

Only it wasn't a possum.

Grrrr.

It was a dog. No, scratch that, it was a three-headed dog, growling in rough harmony. This monster was the size of an Irish wolfhound, with a red-rimmed glare and a mane that moved. One head was wolf, one was Rottweiler, and the third, Chihuahua. (Don't laugh—they're small but vicious.)

My insides turned to posole soup, and my heartbeat hammered like a nail gun in my ears. When I looked closer, I couldn't believe my eyes. That wasn't a mane around its

neck, it was a living collar of what looked like . . . electric eels? Their mouths gaped, and their tiny eyes stared, hungry and remorseless.

"I—I—I . . ." I stuttered, backing into a bush.

"This," said Benny, his voice as tense as a tea party with a tiger, "would be a good time for your distraction."

As we kept edging away from the dog toward the building, I fumbled with clumsy fingers to open my book bag. The creature's six eyes tracked my every move. Its growl ratcheted up, going from the sound of a distant truck to a whole pack of Harleys barreling across your front lawn.

I didn't dare take my eyes off the beast, but I watched, riveted, as ropes of drool descended from two of its mouths. Finally, my hand closed around the tinfoil. With a surge of relief, I dug out the raw hamburger, squeezed it into a ball, and tossed it over the watchdog's head.

"Fetch!" I whispered.

But I hadn't reckoned on the creature's reflexes. It reared onto its hind legs and the wolf head snatched the meat from the air in a gulp. The other two heads snarled and snapped at it, then turned their attention back to us.

"Uh-oh," squeaked Benny.

"You can say that again."

"Uh-oh," he said.

"That's enough, thanks."

Chapter Nineteen

Death Lab
for Cutie

"**G**OT ANY MORE** hamburger?" asked Benny as the three-headed dog stalked toward us.

"No," I said. "Hadn't planned on feeding three mouths."

"What a pity," said a dry voice behind us. "Wan-chan's other heads get so jealous. And that, my young visitors, is a dangerous thing."

Benny and I swiveled to take in this new threat while still keeping an eye on Wan-chan, apparently the dog-creature's name. Unless there was another three-headed monster lurking around here somewhere.

Framed by an open side door stood Haruki Hanzomon, billionaire scientist and general oddball. He wore a royal-purple smoking jacket over ugly sage-green pants. Pouchy, half-lidded eyes examined us with all the emotion of a stone lion in winter.

Benny recovered first. "Uh, hi," he said. "Mind if we come inside for a bit?"

A faint sneer pulled up the billionaire's lip. "Give me one good reason I shouldn't leave you to your fate?"

"Um . . ." Benny's worried glance telegraphed his message: *I got nothing.*

Wan-chan resumed his three-part growling, stalking ever closer. I sucked in a breath, and a crazy inspiration hit me.

"We're the, uh, science heroes of tomorrow," I said, with demented enthusiasm. "And we've come to learn from you."

A corner of Mr. Hanzomon's mouth twitched. It may have been what passed for a smile with this guy. Or it may have been gas. "Most people try the front gate first." His eyes flickered toward the wall we'd scaled. "But I admire your—how do you Americans say? Get-up-and-go."

"Thanks," I said. "We were so excited to see you, we just got up and went."

The scientist stared at us for a painfully long moment before turning and sweeping a hand toward the door. "Please, come inside."

As soon as Benny and I made a move toward safety, the three-headed dog's growls escalated into barks. Its hackles stood up like a tiny dark forest and its eel mane seethed.

"Wan-chan, sit!" snapped Mr. Hanzomon.

Instantly, the fearsome creature plopped down onto his haunches. Those six red-rimmed eyes stayed glued to us, but the barks cut off like a dropped cell-phone call.

That was all the invitation we needed. Benny and I hustled through the door. Behind us, the billionaire murmured, "Who's my good boy?" When I glanced back, he was slipping doggie treats to all three heads.

Why in the world did this billionaire have a monster guard dog? I wondered. Did he collect strange and dangerous things?

Inside, I paused on the gleaming wood floor and took in my surroundings. What can you say about a fancy office? It was smaller than the Palace of Versailles. Barely. And it wasn't quite as flashy as the Taj Mahal. Other than that, it had the usual amount of priceless artwork, expensive furniture, and massive square footage you'd expect from a mind-blowingly expensive facility.

Shutting the door behind him, Mr. Hanzomon inclined his head to us. "Let's go visit the lab, shall we?" Moving stiffly but gracefully, like an ancient panther, he led the way. The faint scent of gardenias trailed in his wake.

"So, uh . . ." I racked my brains for small talk. "Nice dog."

"Wan-chan is very loyal," he said.

"Sweet-tempered, too," I said.

Benny chimed in. "Love the extra heads. More to pet. And the eels? Nice touch. Um, aren't they ocean creatures?"

The scientist's bristly eyebrows rose. "With the proper science, all things are possible."

"Right," I said, realizing with a chill that Mr. Hanzomon was no simple collector of oddities. His research involved messing with living creatures. "Yay, science."

As we passed a side hallway, two black-haired giants in charcoal-gray suits joined us. It took me a while to realize they were women—the kind of women who could wrestle Mrs. Tamasese to a standstill and still have enough energy to subdue a small country.

I suppressed a shudder. Was our host leading us someplace quiet so these amazons could snap our spines like stale churros? Someplace where our blood wouldn't stain the nice floor?

"This way," said Mr. Hanzomon, stepping into an open elevator cab.

I gulped. Too late to back out now.

With the guards crowding behind me, I joined Benny and the scientist in the wood-paneled car. The amazon on the right pressed a button, the doors closed, and we descended so smoothly, you could barely tell we were moving.

When the doors *whoosh*ed open, my jaw practically hit the floor. A vast, shining space stretched out before us, crammed with vats, beakers, test tubes, lasers, operating tables, and mysterious machines. It was like someone had raided a Research-Labs-R-Us store and stocked this place with it.

"Welcome to my little laboratory," said Mr. Hanzomon.

We entered the room. It seemed longer and wider than the building itself, and well equipped enough to make Einstein drool with jealousy.

"I like what you've done with the place," said Benny. "Very science-y."

My gaze fell on a nearby device about the size of a clothing-store changing booth with huge microscopes on either side. "What's this one do?"

Stepping over to it, Mr. Hanzomon stroked the machine like a favorite pet. "The gene splicer," he said. "Care to have the eyes of a fly? Or the legs of a cheetah?"

"Uh, no thanks," I said. "I'm good."

"This machine can make it happen," he said.

I sidled away, feeling clammy. My heartbeat accelerated like a Maserati. Unless he was making a bad joke, this guy had the power to do whatever he wanted with us, to turn us into monsters if he felt like it. And there wasn't a thing we could do.

"Wow," said Benny, running a hand over a centrifuge twice as tall as he was. "You're pretty well stocked. Care to lend a hand with our science project?"

The scientist made a sound like a wombat's wheeze. I

guessed it was a chuckle. "That would be cheating," he said. "Real heroes don't cheat." His half-lidded eyes surveyed us, like he knew exactly what kind of heroes we were hoping to be.

"Uh, right," I said. My gaze rested on an exam table equipped with straps. I suppressed another shudder. "Maybe you could just give us some advice?"

Mr. Hanzomon made a slow nod.

"Our, um, science-fair project is on biotech, and the possibility of doing a mash-up between two animals."

One of the scientist's eyebrows twitched. "'Mash-up'? What is this term?"

"That's when you combine different things together," said Benny helpfully.

"You know, like a cow and a gorilla," I said.

"Or a mosquito and a warthog."

"Or even," I said, "a lion and a scorpion."

I watched closely, but Mr. Hanzomon didn't react. Either his whole face had been Botoxed, or he was one cool customer. "And your question?" he asked.

"We were wondering whether that mash-up would act more like one part of itself than the other?" I said.

The billionaire cocked his head, considering us. "Depends on the creature," he said at last. "And the scientist who created it. For instance, my own private Cerberus, Wan-chan, reacts entirely like a dog, not an eel."

I was interested in spite of myself. "But you could have made him act more eel-like?"

"Certainly. But then he wouldn't be much use as a watchdog."

"Good point," said Benny. "You don't see many watch-eels these days."

I didn't know about my friend, but I felt like I was walking in a minefield. One wrong step, one wrong word, and *kablooie!* Nobody would ever see us again.

"So . . . hypothetically speaking," I said, "if someone wanted to, um, motivate a hybrid creature, he'd have to . . ."

Another dry wheeze. "Try both the carrot and the stick," said Mr. Hanzomon.

"Thanks, but the carrot's probably tastier," said Benny.

"Precisely," said the scientist. He strolled past the exam table. The amazonian guards stayed where they were, arms crossed, blocking the elevator door. There was no other exit. Sweat trickled from my hairline.

"Do you know why I'm so interested in biotech?" the billionaire asked, lifting a scalpel from an instrument tray and toying with it.

"Uh, no," I said.

Sighting along the blade, he said, "Because humanity has grown weak. There are no heroes anymore, just"— he sniffed—"two-faced politicians, self-absorbed YouTube stars, and people famous for being famous."

I thought of my sister, Veronica. But she wasn't just an empty celebrity; she loved acting and was pretty good at it.

"What about athletes?" said Benny, who was crazy about basketball. "They're heroes."

Mr. Hanzomon's lip curled. "Overpaid buffoons playing children's games. How would they perform against a manticore or a Minotaur?"

Light dawned. "Like in Greek myths?" I asked.

The billionaire turned to face us, his eyes kindling with fire. "Perseus, Jason, Atalanta. Now, *those* were heroes."

Benny frowned. "But you know they're mythological, right?"

Mr. Hanzomon continued as if Benny hadn't spoken. "A different age, a better age." Beckoning, he strode toward a series of steel tanks along one wall.

I looked at Benny, who shrugged and followed. I joined him.

"Apart from the obvious, what was the difference between that era and our own?" said the scientist.

"Indoor plumbing?" Benny guessed.

"Deodorant?" I said.

"Worthy foes," said Mr. Hanzomon. He stopped at a waist-high control panel that fronted the tanks. "Theirs was an age of heroes and awesome enemies. But there are no such challenges in our world today, and so, no heroes."

Benny's eyes met mine. No challenges? We could tell

him a thing or two about that. Our lives had been nothing *but* challenges lately.

"And that," said the billionaire, "is why I began Project Gorgon." He pressed several buttons. Panels slid aside in the three closest vats to reveal Plexiglas windows.

Curious, I stepped closer. When I saw what was inside, my knees buckled, and the walls seemed to close in on me.

Mr. Monster's Neighborhood

THE TANKS WERE FULL of monsters.

Each ten-foot-tall vat was packed with reddish goo, like Jell-O, only clearer and more liquid-y. But instead of fruit bits, suspended in this goop was a collection of creatures straight out of nightmare. Giant crabs with human faces. Snakelike beings with bat wings and tiger heads. Humanoids with frog legs and yellow fangs.

And this was only in the three vats we could see. Six more waited behind those.

Hanzomon had the makings of a monster army.

For a brief moment, I thought I would lose my dinner. Folding an arm across my stomach, I nodded toward the snaky things. "Uh, you . . . ?"

"Yes, indeed," said Mr. Hanzomon. The pride in his

voice was as transparent as a shirt made of Scotch tape. "I created them myself—with a little help. Aren't they marvelous?"

Benny looked positively green. "Not exactly the word I was searching for."

The scientist patted the crab creatures' vat. "From a purely scientific point of view, this is a tremendous breakthrough. The next step in humankind's evolution."

"Then why do I feel totally creeped out?" I said.

Mr. Hanzomon turned to face us. An eerie light shone in his eyes. "New ideas seem frightening to the untutored mind."

So do totally loco ideas, I thought.

"And, uh, wha—" Benny cleared his throat. "What are you going to do with the monsters?"

Our host's eyes twinkled. "Why, release them, of course. How else will new heroes emerge, without new monsters to face?"

This guy was going to turn all these monsters loose on our town? Hundreds of people might die. Who knew what damage the creatures would cause. Benny's eyes found mine. I read in them the same thought I was having: *This dude is totally whackadoodle.*

Gingerly, I edged backward. "But why Monterrosa?"

"Yeah, how did we get so lucky?" added Benny.

Spreading his arms, Mr. Hanzomon said, "This place is monster heaven."

"Funny, but they left that slogan off the town's website," said Benny, joining me. I'd noticed that the more nervous he got, the more he tended to joke. Me, too.

The billionaire cocked his head. "It's something about the magnetic field here, ever since that earthquake in October. Quite fascinating. We're not sure why, but the altered resonance encourages abnormality to flourish."

"I can see that," I said, still backing away. His comment explained a lot, actually. About why we'd had to tangle with were-hyenas, mutant mantises, and scorp-lions—all between Halloween and Christmas.

But that didn't change one essential fact: he was still nuttier than the contents of a squirrel's lunch box.

"So?" Mr. Hanzomon indicated the laboratory. "What do you think?"

"Words can't express what I think," I said.

Stroking his chin, the scientist said, "You know, this is a big project, and I recently lost my assistant. I could use some reliable interns with a passion for science. Interested?"

"Gee," said Benny. "Sorry, but my pee-wee football league starts next week."

I gestured toward the elevator. "And we really should be getting home."

"Of course," said our host.

I blinked. Was he really going to let us walk out, after all we'd seen? Benny and I stood just a few feet away from the elevator doors. The guards still blocked our path.

"So we can go?" said Benny.

"Certainly," said the scientist.

"Just like that?" I asked.

He did that twitchy thing with his mouth that passed for a smile. "You two said you want to be heroes."

I flinched. Me and my big mouth . . .

"My people have been monitoring events at your school," said the scientist. "They told me how you responded to the creatures I sent there."

A jolt raced through my limbs. "So you *are* the source of the scorp-lions."

"Yes."

"Oh, man." Benny wiped his forehead. "You couldn't have sent a mash-up of a bunny and a baby duck instead?"

Mr. Hanzomon ignored him, clasping his hands behind his back. "You want to be heroes, here's your chance."

"How do you mean?" asked Benny.

"If you can make it past my pets and over the wall, you will have proven yourselves heroic enough to leave. If not . . ." The scientist made a careless gesture. "Oh, well."

I didn't much like the sound of *oh, well*, or of his "pets." But I was afraid if we stayed there much longer, Mr. Hanzomon would try giving us giraffe necks or hawk feet. Keeping wary eyes on the billionaire, we approached the elevator.

At a nod from Mr. Hanzomon, the giant guards moved aside. "Release Fluffy and her kittens," he said. Amazon

Number One went to a control panel on the wall and flipped a switch.

Benny tried to chuckle. "Fluffy?"

"We'll see if you're still laughing when you meet her," said our host.

We stepped into the open car and pushed the button for the ground floor.

"In case I never see you alive again," said Mr. Hanzomon, "it's been . . . interesting. If you're the best your school has to offer, the new age of heroes may be off to a slow start."

I blurted, "Oh yeah? Well, you have terrible taste in pants." The doors shut.

"Terrible taste in pants?" said Benny.

"It takes me a while to come up with good insults," I said.

As the car rose, we checked our book bags. The contents of mine weren't very reassuring: a flashlight, several hard-boiled eggs, a PowerBar, and one of Zeppo's old tennis balls. "I hope you've still got your distraction," I said. "We might need it."

Benny flashed me a thumbs-up. Then the elevator stopped and the doors slid open. Showtime.

We poked our heads out. The hallway lay empty, as quiet as midnight at the morgue.

"Which way to the door?" whispered Benny.

I pointed right. "This way, I think."

"Let's go."

Both of us walked tiptoe, carrying our bags in one hand, braced for the slightest threat. My head swiveled. My muscles were as tight as Green Arrow's bowstring.

Past one high-tech office after another we went. One room was entirely lined with floor-to-ceiling bookshelves, another with racks of animal figurines. A clock ticked down the hall. A faint buzzing came from somewhere nearby. But everything else was still.

The farther we went, the more my heart tried to climb out through my throat. We were crazy—no, worse than crazy. Two fourth graders trying to be heroes? It was ridiculous. I couldn't even keep my parents together; how could I imagine that Benny and I might save our town from monsters?

We paused at a cross-corridor, listening intently. Fancy track lighting cast little spotlights on various gold-framed paintings. A potted ficus shed a leaf. That was all.

"What do you suppose Fluffy is?" I whispered.

"If Wan-chan is anything to go by," said Benny, "a total freakazoid."

"Wonderful," I said.

We made it past another few offices without incident. At the next intersection, we stopped again. The buzzing was louder now, like the inside of an enormous beehive. The sound seemed to come from everywhere, and I knew it couldn't possibly mean anything good. The pit of my stomach felt emptier than a bully's compliment.

"Maybe it's a snore," whispered Benny. "Maybe Fluffy's sleeping."

"Maybe."

Somehow, I didn't think we'd be quite that lucky.

As we stood looking down the other corridor, a droplet landed on my neck. I reached to brush it off while glancing up for the source.

My blood froze. Directly above me, clinging to the ceiling, was a new kind of horror. The head and body were that of an enormous tabby cat, big as a lynx. But from that body extended eight hairy spider legs, which gripped the ceiling.

Another drop of drool fell on me.

"¡D-D-Dios mío!" I choked out, pointing upward.

"Yikes." Benny's eyes went round as softballs. "N-n-nice kitty?" he crooned.

With a sinking feeling, I realized that the buzzing was coming from this mutant creature. She was purring, probably over the thought of dinner.

And that dinner was *me*.

Chapter Twenty-One

Bright Lights, Big Kitty

TWO ENORMOUS AMBER eyes stared down at us, unblinking. A gooey strand shot out from somewhere near Fluffy's butt. Webbing.

I dodged, and it hit the wall beside me.

Benny's hand dipped into his book bag and emerged with a massive squirt gun. He fired a stream at the spider-cat.

The monster hissed and recoiled.

"Run!" he cried.

I didn't need an engraved invitation. Turning, I dashed down the hall with Benny at my heels.

"You brought a squirt gun?" I said.

"You didn't?" asked Benny.

As we pelted down the corridor, I realized that we should have reached the side door by now. The hallway ended in a sunken break room as big as my entire house. We skidded to a stop.

Uh-oh.

"Where's the danged exit?" said Benny.

"We must have gotten turned around." I glanced behind. Fluffy was scuttling along the wall toward us with jaws open wide. *"Yaah!"*

"No fair!" cried Benny. "She's got eight legs, we've got two."

We charged across the break room, using a leather sofa as a trampoline and going airborne. I didn't quite stick my landing, though—a lamp and side table crashed to the floor. Toward the far end of the room, I spied another hall entrance.

"This way!" I cried.

We leaped up the steps and barreled around a blind corner—straight into a mass of sticky strands.

"Eeugh!" Benny fought to free himself. I struggled. The fibers were as gooey as a cobweb, but a whole lot stronger.

A flash of movement from above drew my eye. Clinging to the ceiling and upper wall were three smaller versions of Fluffy.

I pointed. "Spider-kittens!"

Benny angled his squirt gun and blasted away. The creatures hissed, scuttling backward. And then his gun ran out of water. "Whoops."

Something made me turn my head. Behind us, scrambling

over the break room furniture, was Fluffy. And she clearly didn't like how we were treating her babies.

I elbowed Benny. "We're surrounded. Will your big distraction work on spider-cats?"

"Let's find out." His book bag was hopelessly snarled in the web, so he focused on unzipping it. While he worked, the kittens started creeping back. Mama Fluffy continued her steady advance.

"Anytime now." I freed my other arm. Good thing this web wasn't woven by anything bigger, or we'd never escape.

Benny shoved several items into my hands.

"Fireworks?" I said. "Indoors? That's super-dangerous!"

He fumbled with matches. "Would you rather be dinner?"

"Fireworks it is," I said.

As soon as Benny lit the fuse to the ground spinner, I set it down and kicked it along the floor toward Fluffy. She stopped, wary of the crackling sound. Her tail lashed the air.

We set the cone and the missile rocket on the ground, pointing roughly toward the spider kittens. The fuses sizzled. The creatures watched, fascinated.

Frantically, Benny and I wrenched our limbs and bodies away from the sticky spiderweb. I didn't want to find out what happened when a rocket went off almost under your feet.

At last, we freed ourselves. "Go, go, go!" Benny yelled.

I yanked my book bag free of the web and followed him toward the break room.

The spinner went off first. Red, then yellow, then blue sparks fountained as it whirled. With a yowl, Fluffy headed for the hills. All that fur standing on end made her look a bit like an enormous, eight-legged hedgehog.

Sparks stung my bare calves as Benny and I dodged past the firework. I glanced back.

With a sensational *ka-POW*, the cone exploded in a rainbow of light. Beside it, the missile boomed and launched, lodging itself in the ceiling near where the kittens had been. But they were long gone. At the first explosion, they'd retreated down the hallway in a blur.

A smoke alarm wailed like a baby ghoul with a wet diaper. Ceiling sprinklers blasted into action.

"Over here!" Benny called from a corner of the room. "The front door!"

When I joined him, I noticed an alcove we'd missed earlier. It led to enormous double doors whose frosted glass was set with wrought-iron scrollwork.

"¡Híjole!" I sighed. "About time."

We blasted through the doors into the cool night air. An earsplitting burglar alarm added its voice to the din, but I didn't mind. My spirits soared. We'd escaped Mr. Hanzomon's pets!

Pounding down the flagstone path, Benny and I headed

for the circular driveway. We were in the home stretch now.

But just as we hit the bricks, a furious barking arose from behind us.

The three-headed dog!

Around the corner of the house he raced, galloping along with alarming speed. All three heads glared at us, fangs bared.

"Not fair!" cried Benny.

I eyeballed the distant gate. The billionaire's headquarters had way too much driveway; we'd never escape before Wan-chan caught us. And no handy trees grew nearby.

Grabbing Benny's arm, I said, "Wait."

"Are you crazy?" he cried. "He'll eat us up!"

I dug into my bag, and my hand closed around the hard-boiled eggs. "Here." Handing him an egg, I took the other two for myself.

"Three eggs won't stop Wan-chan," said Benny.

"No, but they might slow him down. When I give the word, toss yours a couple feet to the right."

The monster dog bore down on us. With each step, I could see more detail, and the details scared the fajitas out of me.

"Wait," said Benny. "I throw to my right or his right?"

"Your right."

Wan-chan was only ten feet away. His reddish eyes glowed in the security lights. His legs were a blur of movement.

"Wan-chan!" I yelled. "Fetch!"

I tossed one egg to the creature's left, and one egg above him, out of reach. Benny's sailed off to his right. I held my breath. This was either the dumbest idea in the world, or . . .

The huge dog put on the brakes, skidding across the brick. Each head surged in a different direction—the Rottweiler to the left, the wolf behind, and the Chihuahua to the right. Confused by three different sets of orders, the body twisted first this way, then that, as the heads tried to claim their prizes.

The Chihuahua snapped at the wolf, the Rottweiler lunged at the Chihuahua. Fur flew.

We were totally forgotten.

I tapped Benny on the shoulder. Laying a finger across my lips for quiet, I motioned toward the gate. We speed walked down the driveway. As we began scaling the gate, I glanced back. Wan-chan was still struggling with himself.

"How did you know?" asked Benny as we climbed.

"Same technique you use with your parents," I said. "Divide and conquer."

The Scream
Team

NERVES STILL JANGLING from our close call, I reached home just as the first glimmer of dawn touched the sky. I was burning to tell someone about Monterrosa's own Dr. Frankenstein. But as I eased through the back door, a more immediate concern took over. Something clattered in a nearby room. My dad was up!

I hustled into the kitchen, hoping to make it to my bedroom before he saw me. No such luck. Around the corner he shuffled, bed-haired and stubble-cheeked.

"Carlos," he said, dark eyes serious, "we need to talk."

I froze. "Uh." I was thoroughly busted, and my dad was about to ground me until I was a grandparent.

"I, uh, I'm sorry?" I said.

His frown was puzzled. "For what?"

I caught myself. Was it possible he didn't know I'd sneaked out? "Um, for . . . drinking milk straight from the carton," I said. "What did you want to talk about?"

"It's your mom and sister."

I gripped the back of a chair. "What's wrong? Are they okay?"

"Yes. No. They're fine," said my dad. "They're coming home tonight."

"Tonight?"

Veronica's winter break on the TV show was almost a week away. Why would they come home . . . ? Suddenly it felt like a lead muffin had landed in my stomach. Were my mom and dad so eager to get divorced they couldn't wait a week?

"Are we—I mean, are you—?" I began.

My dad stepped close and kissed me on the top of my head. "Gotta run, *chamaco*. I'm late for an early meeting. Your *abuela* will take you to school."

"But—"

He spun and hurried toward the bathroom, calling, "Don't worry, we'll talk about it tonight."

I sighed. That was exactly what I was afraid of.

Benny met me by the flagpole just before school. I'd convinced him that we needed to tell Principal Johnson about the monster lab, and he'd convinced me that we had to edit our story a bit if we didn't want to use up our last detention passes. Kids swirled around us as we headed for the office. And out of that swirl stepped Esme Ygorre.

"So?" she said. "Did you find my mom's ex-boss?"

Benny glanced at me. "Yeah," he said.

"You could say that," I added.

"And?" She leaned in close, half whispering. "Did he have any cool monsters?"

At the mention of monsters, my hands trembled. "If you call a three-headed dog that tries to eat you 'cool,'" I said, "then, yeah."

"Awesome," she breathed. "I'd love one of those. But Mom won't let me."

Benny sent her a deadpan look. "Your life is so hard," he said.

"I know," she agreed, oblivious to his sarcasm.

The flow of students around us was slowing to a trickle. We'd have to hustle if we wanted to talk to Mrs. Johnson before class started.

"Look," said Benny, "we've got an important meeting with the principal, so would you mind—?"

Esme bounced on her toes. "Does the meeting have anything to do with monsters?"

"Maybe," I said.

"Then I'm your girl," she said. "I know all about them."

"I'm sure you do," said Benny. "But we don't want to hear about your dating life."

I put a hand on his arm. "Hang on. She helped us find Hanzomon. Maybe she can help with the scorp-lions."

"Those are the ones with the cute curly tails?" asked Esme.

Benny's lips compressed into a thin line. "Can we talk?" he asked me.

"Excuse us," I told Esme.

She waved a hand airily and fiddled with her book-bag strap.

Benny led me a few steps away. "What are you thinking?" he whispered.

"That she can help," I said.

"But this is *our* thing," he said. "We're the heroes. We've got to go it alone."

"Says who?" I asked. "The hero handbook?"

He counted off on his fingers. "Okay, let's talk about superheroes. Thor, Hulk, Batman, Spider-Man? All of 'em work alone or with a partner."

I folded my arms. "And the Avengers and Fantastic Four are both teams."

"But we're doing great, just the two of us."

"Seriously? You believe that?"

He tried for a smile. "Sure. We found out it wasn't a haunting; we found out who made the scorp-lions. Progress."

I wagged my head. "But we haven't gotten rid of the

monsters. Look, I'm not saying we should quit, just that we get some help. Mrs. T backed us up before."

"Yeah, but her?" Benny glared at Esme, who was making some kind of weird beat-box sounds with her lips. "She's a little too into monsters."

"So are we," I said.

"But we want to fight them," said Benny. "She wants to take them home and feed them a Milk Bone."

"True." I spread my hands. "But maybe that's exactly what we need. A new angle."

Benny looked at me, then at Esme. He pinched his bottom lip. "Okay," he said at last. "But don't blame me if she tries to put the monsters in a stroller and play house."

I blew out some air in relief. "Deal."

And wouldn't you know it? That's just when the bell decided to ring.

"Come on!" I told Esme, breaking into a sprint for our classroom.

"But what about the monsters?" She hustled along behind us, book bag jouncing.

"Fill you in at recess," said Benny.

After all the drama I'd experienced lately, I was relieved that Mr. Chu's lessons were uneventful. We studied the water cycle, we completed our Greek helmets and shields. But even though nobody fell into a coma, our class remained as jittery as a sackful of Super Balls on a trampoline.

Everyone knew something was wrong. Everyone was waiting for disaster.

And the weather didn't help. It rained all morning, so we had indoor recess in Mr. Chu's classroom. Benny and I set up some old board game called Operation, and Esme sidled up to us to continue our conversation.

"So?" she said. "Spill."

"We're trying to get rid of the scorp-lions," I said, "but they're pretty well dug in." I ran down our efforts so far. When I finished, she steepled her fingers.

"I see your problem right there," she said.

"We're just too macho?" said Benny, flexing his biceps.

Esme gave him the kind of smile that says, *You're so not funny, but I'm too polite to mention it.* "Kind of," she said. "You've been trying to force them out, right?"

"Well, yeah," I said. "That's sort of the point."

She shook her head. *"Lure* them out instead."

"How?" said Benny. "By dressing up as a girl monster? We don't even know if these things are boys, girls, or neither of the above."

"Ahh." The light went on in the fridge that was my brain. "Use the carrot, not the stick."

"Exactly," said Esme.

Benny slid his chair closer. "Like that Hanzomon guy said? But how do we do that?"

Sensing a presence behind me, I turned my head.

"By getting your friends to lend a hand," said Tina

Green. She pulled up a chair and straddled it. "Now, what's the plan, and how can I help?"

Come lunchtime, the four of us had our tasks. Of course, Benny and I assigned ourselves one of the toughest—convincing Principal Johnson to do her part.

"And why in blue blazes would I tell Animal Control to come *after* school?" she said when we cornered her outside the teachers' lunchroom. "They'll be here in half an hour."

"Because that'll be their best chance to catch the monsters," said Benny.

Mrs. Johnson crossed her arms. "Mm-hmm. And you know this how?"

I glanced over at Benny. "We've, uh, done some research."

"Research," she repeated, eyeing us. "Why do I get the feeling you've been disobeying my direct orders?"

"Honest." Benny raised his palm as if swearing an oath. "We haven't gone anywhere off-limits since you told us not to."

Except maybe Mr. Hanzomon's office, I thought. But I saw no reason to burden her with that knowledge quite yet.

"It's true," I said. "Would you please, *please* tell Animal Control to set up their cages in the hall outside the multipurpose room?"

"After school," Benny added.

Our principal frowned. "But that's so close to where

we're holding the science fair. The risk—I don't know. . . ."

"Please?" said Benny and I together. We gave her the full Bambi-eyes treatment.

Mrs. Johnson fired off the Principal Stare in return, but we didn't flinch. "I'm not your parents," she said. "You can't just beg me until I give in."

We gazed at her, unblinking.

"I have my students' safety to consider," she said.

Benny and I stared some more.

She scowled. "Nothing you say is going to make me forget my responsibility."

"Everybody will be inside, and the monsters will be outside," I said. "What could be safer?"

"But I can't—"

Assuming his most serious expression, Benny said, "Mrs. Johnson, with all due respect, this is our school's last chance. Animal Control doesn't know these creatures. We do."

"And we can keep the school from being shut down," I said.

The stress of the past few days showed in our principal's expression and the circles under her eyes. She searched our faces, weighing our words.

"Plus," I said, "we've solved other monster problems before. So really, we're more experienced at this than Animal Control."

Mrs. Johnson's face softened, and for a moment, it wasn't

principal-to-student, it was just person-to-person. "Why?" she asked. "Why on God's green earth do you rush into something everyone else would rather avoid?"

Several answers came to mind, from the flip ("We need more get-out-of-detention-free passes") to the mock-deep ("Because it's there"). In the end, I settled on the truth.

"Sometimes, someone's just got to step up," I said. "No matter whether they're a total hero or a regular person. This is our time."

Benny jerked a thumb at me. "What he said."

Eyes unfocused, our principal nodded slowly. Then her gaze sharpened. "Here's what's going to happen. I'll make sure Animal Control is there at the right place and time."

"Great!" said Benny.

"And you two will take all possible safety precautions. You will let the professionals handle the creatures. You will not put yourselves or any other students in danger. Are we clear?"

"As crystal," I said.

We settled a few details. Before Mrs. Johnson left to call Animal Control, she said, "I'm taking a big risk here. I sincerely hope you know what you're doing."

Benny and I nodded solemnly.

So do we, I thought. So do we.

Chapter Twenty-Three

Scorp-Lions, Bunnies, and Bears, Oh My!

THE REST OF that afternoon was as pleasant and restful as a stroll through an active volcano. Worries ran in circles through my head. Would Tina and Esme hold up their end of things? Was Esme right about the monsters' reactions? Would our harebrained scheme actually work? And, oh yeah, would my parents announce their divorce at dinner that night?

To say that I was a bit distracted would be like calling the Revolutionary War a little spat between friends. It didn't quite cover the subject.

Despite all this, Benny and I did manage to put the

finishing touches—except for a last few—on our science-fair project. At long last, the final bell rang.

"Listen up, my fellow scientists," said Mr. Chu. He was decked out as a mad genius, complete with goggles, Einstein wig, and lab coat. "The hour has come. Everyone who's participating, I want you to carefully carry your projects to the multipurpose room. Best of luck, and may you blind them with . . ."

"Science!" everyone shouted.

Mr. Chu beamed. I guessed he really liked that old song.

My classmates collected their poster boards and various project materials. Benny assembled ours, which was pretty skimpy. I gathered up our Greek helmets and shields—made extra thick for better protection.

"Uh, Carlos," said Mr. Chu, "you do know it's not a history fair, don't you?"

"Absolutely," I said. "But if I don't bring them, we'll *be* history."

Our teacher quirked an eyebrow at that but made no further comment. Overhearing us, Tyler Spork said, "They're probably doing 'The Miracle of Papier-Mâché.'" He snickered nastily, until Benny mouthed the words *double-dog dare*. That made him shut up in a hurry.

I smiled. It was so sweet to have something to hold over Tyler, I thought we might delay his dare until the end of the year.

Amid all the hubbub, Tina edged up to me and slipped

a key into my palm. "There you go," she said. "And if you're caught, I have no idea how you got it."

"Thanks, Karate Girl," I said. "But how did *you* get it?"

Tina sent me a level look. "I could tell you," she said. "But then I'd have to kill you."

I knew she was kidding. Sort of.

Pocketing the key, I joined Benny and the flow of kids heading down the covered hallway. I hadn't taken three steps before I spotted Esme skulking behind a post.

"Psst," she hissed.

Rolling my eyes, I went over to her. "It's no big secret. You could just say, 'Hey, Carlos.'"

"I know," she said, "but my way's more fun. Here." She handed me two jumbo-sized stuffed toys—a blue bear and a bucktoothed pink rabbit that smelled faintly of mint and lemongrass.

"Um, thanks," I said. "Friends of yours?"

She glanced both ways, then muttered, "We put the stuff inside 'em. You know, to activate the predator instinct."

"Ah." I tucked the toys under my arms. "Well, thanks."

"Sure you don't need me to come along?"

I shook my head. "Better not. If this goes sour, we don't want anyone else getting in trouble." Besides, I couldn't be sure she wouldn't try to pet the scorp-lions when they appeared.

Esme wished us luck and dashed back to our room to collect her project.

When we reached the multipurpose room, the place was as hopping as a kangaroo farm at chow time. Kids from all three upper grades milled about, setting up their projects on the tables, chatting with friends, and trash-talking the competition. I saw model volcanoes and lemon batteries, a Mentos-cola geyser and a static-electricity experiment. One project was called "Can Goldfish Do Tricks?" and another, "Garlic: The Silent Killer."

When it came to science, Monterrosa students had all bases covered.

PTA volunteers and a handful of workers in sky-blue Hanzomon jumpsuits lent a hand here and there. With a start, I realized that the mad billionaire himself was supposed to be one of the judges. My legs went shaky.

"Do you see him anywhere?" I asked Benny as we set up our table.

"Who?" he asked.

"Mr. Hanzomon. If he interferes with us, we're toast."

"Don't worry." Benny smirked. "Even he's not loony enough to try anything with witnesses around."

"You sure?" I twisted my hands. "We're talking about a guy with a three-headed dog and spider-cats."

Benny wagged his head, acknowledging my point. "Okay, okay. He's nutty enough to unleash Armageddon right here, just to see if any 'heroes arise.' Satisfied?"

He was joking, but fingers of anxiety tickled along my spine. What if the scientist *did* step in to help his freaky creations? Or unleash some of the nightmares from his basement lab? People could get hurt. *We* could get hurt.

I spotted Mrs. Johnson across the room greeting parents and soothing junior scientists. After threading my way through the crowd, I shifted from foot to foot, waiting for her to stop talking. Setting down the stuffed rabbit, I raised my hand.

"What is it, Carlos?" she said. "I'm busier than a gopher on a golf course."

"It's about the you-know-whats," I said.

Excusing herself, the principal pulled me aside. "Has something happened?"

"Not yet," I said, "but something might."

"Tell me."

I pressed my palms together. "Please stick close to Mr. Hanzomon. Don't let him out of your sight."

Her forehead crinkled. "Mr. Hanzomon? Our sponsor?"

"Yes, we're afraid he might get involved if he sees the creatures. We don't want him inter—uh, we don't want him getting hurt."

"Don't worry." She patted my shoulder. "I'll protect him."

Not quite what I meant, but at least she'd keep an eye on the guy.

The principal looked down at my two huge stuffed toys. "Aren't you a little old for lovies?"

My cheeks went warm. "It's . . . for our project."

At that moment, voices rose at the big double doors. Mrs. Johnson spun. "Ah, speak of the devil."

Truer words were never spoken. For there, surrounded by blue-suited flunkies and PTA well-wishers, was the mad king of mad scientists himself, Haruki Hanzomon. Calling a greeting, Mrs. Johnson headed his way.

Just by chance, our eyes met. His gaze burned into mine like hot coals on balsa wood. His index finger tapped at the corner of one eye—*I'm watching you*—and then he turned to meet the principal.

A shiver rippled through me. I hated that I didn't know what the billionaire might do, but it was too late to turn back now. Sucking it up, I hustled over to Benny.

"They're about to start," I said. "Come on."

"At last." He beat his chest. "This dude is ready to kick some scorp-lion tail."

I passed him the rabbit toy. "And here's what you'll do it with."

Benny cocked his head. "Right. Because nothing says superhero like a three-foot-tall pink bunny."

Hefting the blue bear, I looped a length of twine around its neck. Benny did the same with his bunny. We donned our Greek helmets and shields, and brought along a can of soda, just for insurance.

"Hero time," I said.

Benny and I turned and strode out the side door,

dragging our giant stuffed animals behind us. I knew we must look totally ridiculous.

"Hey, look, it's—" Tyler began. But with one glare from us, he shut up.

A smile tugged at my lips. That was me: a tough guy with a teddy bear.

Outside, the hallways were deserted, like a Wild West town before the big showdown. Through the chain-link fence, Benny and I spotted the Animal Control team pulling gear from their truck. I patted my pocket and felt the key.

Everything was ready. But were we?

The closer we drew to the mechanical room, the faster my heart beat. In just a few minutes, we'd either be school heroes or in a deep coma.

"You're not nervous, are you?" I asked.

"Me? Nah." Benny blinked rapidly. "You?"

I swallowed. "Chill as a cucumber sandwich."

We marched right up to the room, and I fitted Tina's key into the lock. "Here goes nothing," I said.

And then I opened the door.

Chapter Twenty-Four

You Can't Hide Your Lion Eyes

CREAKING LIKE A COFFIN LID, the mechanical room's door swung open onto darkness. The stink of a million litter boxes on a hot day rushed out, hitting us full force.

"Oh, man," gasped Benny. "That's all kinds of nasty."

I fanned the air. "It's okay, I wasn't using my nose anyway."

It smelled like the scorp-lions had really made themselves at home. Switching on the fluorescent lights, we stepped into the room.

Everything seemed pretty much the same as on our last visit, but a whole lot stenchier. I tried breathing through my mouth. Nerves stretched taut, Benny and I crept down the aisle beside the boilers, holding up our shields and stuffed toys, and scanning for danger.

Nothing behind the first boiler. Or the second.

Then we passed the third tank, and a wave of goose pimples swept my body. For there, lapping at two saucers of milk, were the four scorp-lions. Eight cat eyes turned our way. Four scorpion tails rose in threat. One of the monsters rumbled.

"Where'd they get the milk?" said Benny.

"I'm guessing Tina."

He cleared his throat. "Sweet of her."

"The sweetest." I licked dry lips. "But now we've got to draw them away from it without ticking them off."

"Piece of cake," said Benny.

Buzzing with adrenaline, I took a couple of steps toward the monsters. They growled and crouched lower. I froze.

"Is it my imagination," I said, "or have they grown?"

"Oh yeah," said Benny. "They're bigger."

Since we'd last seen them, the larger two monsters had swelled from the size of a pit bull to that of a Doberman. The smaller two were now as big as the others had been before. Singly, they could cause serious damage. Together? They were practically unstoppable.

"Hope they like the lure," said Benny. Grabbing his stuffed bunny by the ears, he chucked it into the space between us and them—keeping tight hold of the leash.

Instantly, the growling stopped. The scorp-lions sniffed the air. They sniffed some more. Then their cat eyes grew big as amber moons, staring at the stuffed animal. The milk was forgotten.

"Funny," I said, "how catnip gets a cat's attention."

Good old Esme. With the help of her mother, she had stuffed a boatload of the herb into each of the toys.

The biggest scorp-lion slunk forward a couple of paces toward the bunny. Benny tugged on the cord, dragging it backward. Rising, the other three monsters followed their leader.

Benny backed up. "Heeere, stinging kitties," he crooned. "Nice kitties."

I tossed my stuffed bear beside his toy, and two of the scorp-lions fixated on it. Step-by-step, we made our way toward the door, dragging the bait with us.

Step-by-step, the scorp-lions followed. Desperate to catch up with the catnip, the biggest one pounced.

"Yikes!" cried Benny. Reeling backward, he jerked the cord, twitching the stuffed toy out of range.

I retreated with him. After nailing my shoulder on one of the boilers, I tried to split my attention between the path behind and the monsters ahead. It wasn't easy.

The scorp-lions stalked forward, picking up their pace.

"They're quick!" I said.

The creatures began emitting a low moaning sound that thoroughly creeped me out. One of them got close enough

to snatch at the stuffed bear with its pincer. I tugged the toy away.

That was all we needed. If the monsters seized the bait before we could lure them outdoors, we'd never get them out of this place.

"Almost there," said Benny.

I checked behind us. We were nearly at the exit, and still managing to keep just out of the scorp-lions' reach.

"Easy does it." I stepped through the doorway.

And then, Benny's foot tangled in my leash, and he lost his balance. With hands full, he couldn't catch himself. *Bam!* His head smacked into the doorframe, and he went down hard.

"Benny!"

The scorp-lions surged toward the toys and my fallen friend. I tensed. Somehow, I had to save both Benny and our plan.

From deep down in my gut, the word *"No!"* erupted like a volcano. I lunged forward. With one hand, I yanked the leashes as hard as I could, hauling the toys across the threshold. With the other, I braced my shield over Benny.

The monsters snarled.

"Back, you catnip-sucking freaks!" I cried, feinting with the shield. The biggest monster clacked his front pincers and whipped his tail forward like a lash.

Pummf! The stinger punctured my papier-mâché shield, an inch above my arm.

"*¡Ay huey!*" So much for ancient Greek protection. Too late, I wished Benny and I had made ourselves some swords. Real swords. I crouched over him, shaking his shoulder.

He moaned.

"Come on, dude," I said. "No time for napping."

The frustrated scorp-lions roared, gathering themselves for a charge. I braced myself. No way around it—we were done for.

"Squirt gun," Benny mumbled. "Pocket."

Fumbling his weapon free, I blasted it at the closest monsters. When the water hit, they hissed, recoiling. But they were no spider-cats. It would only buy us a few seconds.

I jammed the squirt gun into my waistband, got a hand under Benny's armpit, and lugged him to his feet. "Let's go, Sleeping Beauty."

He groaned and retrieved his shield. "Stupid doorframe. My head hurts."

"If we don't motor, that won't be the only thing hurting." I guided Benny outdoors, shoving his leash into his hand. "Tell me you can walk."

He took a couple of steps, as graceful as a baby giraffe on ice. "I can walk."

"Good enough for me. Let's go."

As soon as we'd cleared the doorway, one of the scorp-lions stuck its head and pincers outside. It cringed, daunted by the late-afternoon sunlight.

Jerking the cord to make the stuffed bear twitch

and dance, I cried, "Don't wimp out now! Fresh catnip. Num-num!"

That did it. The creature focused on the bear again. It began doing that wiggly-butt stalking thing that cats do, and I waited until just before it pounced to yank the toy away. The monster followed, mesmerized.

Behind it, the other three scorp-lions emerged, blinking, into the daylight. They zeroed in on Benny's bunny.

"Can you run yet?" I asked him.

He grimaced. "Maybe a fast stumble."

"That'll have to do."

Up the covered corridor we led them, like the Pied Pipers of Monterrosa, toward the multipurpose room. When we sped up, the monsters sped up. When they pounced, we twitched the stuffed toys out of their grasp.

Slanting rays of sunshine turned the wet grass to emerald and sparkled off the creatures' armored backs. It would've almost been pretty, if they hadn't been highly dangerous freaks of nature.

With the shields on our arms and the deadly scorp-lions stalking us, I had a brief flash of how those ancient Greek heroes might have felt. Noble, strong, and scared out of their wits.

But all was going well enough, until . . .

"Oh, they're so *cute*!"

Esme showed up.

Chapter Twenty-Five

Science Friction

SHE POPPED OUT behind us like a Goth jack-in-the-box just as we turned the corner to the multipurpose room. "Look at those fluffy ears and curly tails," Esme gushed. "You didn't tell me these monsters were *this* adorable."

"They're not," Benny said.

"Get back!" I cried.

"But just look at them." She sidled around me for a better view.

I glanced behind us. Past her, maybe thirty feet away, stood the cages. Two Animal Control workers waited beside them, horrified and fascinated.

So close. And yet . . .

"Esme," I said, "you promised you'd stay away."

She lifted a shoulder, flashing an apologetic grin. "I fibbed. Mom almost never lets me see her monsters, so I couldn't resist the chance to check them out."

One of the scorp-lions snarled, disturbed by Esme's presence. Distracted, the others peered her way.

I jerked the teddy bear in front of them. "Come on. Keep those pincers pointed at me."

The monsters' gaze went from Esme to the toy and back. But the catnip's aroma was stronger than their curiosity. They resumed stalking.

"Aw, do we have to give them to Animal Control?" she whined as the three of us backed up the hallway.

Benny shot me a superior look. "I hate to say 'I told you so,' but—no, wait, I love to say it. I told you so!"

"These aren't pet hamsters," I told Esme, watching the scorp-lions. "They've already put a bunch of people in the hospital."

"Yeah, but—" she said.

"Esme, no!" I snapped. Too late. She had slipped around me and was approaching the nearest scorp-lion, hand held out to pet it. Esme dodged my grab.

"That's a sweet monst—" she began.

In an impressive display, the creature bared its fangs, clacked its pincers, and hissed, tail held high.

Esme recoiled. "Naughty scorp-lion," she scolded. "I'm your friend."

It roared. Down lashed the scorpion tail, and I gritted

my teeth. But Esme was quicker than she looked. Ducking under its strike, she dodged out of harm's way.

"Well!" she huffed. "You're a rude little thing."

I'd been so focused on her near disaster that I'd neglected to keep the stuffed toy out of reach. Seizing its chance, the lead scorp-lion pounced on the teddy bear.

"No!" I cried.

The monster pinned its prey with one paw and began rubbing its shaggy head against the fabric, purring like a beehive on a honey high. I hauled on the cord, but the scorp-lion was too strong. The bear was trapped.

I growled in frustration. If we didn't get these creatures locked up pronto, they'd go dig in someplace new, stinging people right and left.

"Leave it!" I feinted with my shield at the scorp-lion's head.

A hiss, and that needle-sharp tail came plunging down at me again. Once more, I blocked it with my shield—just barely. A drop of poison sizzled on my skin.

We were locked in a standoff. I snatched a glance at Benny. He kept his bunny moving, but I could tell he didn't want to lure the monsters past and let them get behind me. We were running out of time.

"Bad monster!" Before I knew it, Tina darted in from out of nowhere, and smacked the scorp-lion on the nose with a fistful of rolled-up science-fair programs. It flinched, more surprised than hurt.

I twitched the toy away. "Thanks, Karate Girl."

"What are friends for?" she said.

I grinned. "Now stand back."

For once, she listened. As Tina retreated up the hall with us, I heard Esme telling her, "But they looked so friendly . . ."

One of Benny's monsters briefly snagged his stuffed toy with its claw, but he tugged the bunny free before the creature claimed it. The monsters were growing tired of our teasing. They wanted their sweet-smelling treat, and they wanted it now.

Time to wrap this up.

"Homestretch," I told Benny, making the teddy bear dance out of reach.

"Homestretch," he echoed. But I could tell he was still a bit dizzy.

Step-by-step, feint by feint, we led the scorp-lions toward their cages. They pounced, they batted, and they moaned, drawn to the catnip like kids to Christmas candy.

Ten feet from the cage doors, I whirled, ready to chuck the teddy bear inside. And who should be blocking my way but Mr. Haruki Hanzomon.

"Don't do this," I said. "Please." No reason to be rude, just because he'd tried to feed us to his pets.

"Tricks and traps," he scoffed. "You are afraid to face the monsters in hand-to-hand combat."

"Heck, yeah, we're afraid," I said, keeping the bear moving.

"They're monsters, we're kids," Benny said.

The billionaire sniffed. "Age doesn't matter to a true hero."

"Hey, mister," said one Animal Control worker. "You should move."

"I won't," he said.

"Get out of the way!" I snapped, abandoning all politeness.

"No," said Mr. Hanzomon. "Now what will you do?"

I glanced at the scorp-lions. They were closing in.

Benny and I backed up until we were right in front of the scientist—caught between the madman and his monsters. We had to think fast. Something about Greek myths popped into my head.

"Hang on," I said. "Heroes used trickery all the time. What about that guy who blinded the Cyclops? He sneaked out of his cave under a sheep."

"Yeah," said Benny. "And that dude who answered the Sphinx's riddle, forcing her to jump off a cliff. They didn't duke it out."

"Cheaters," said Mr. Hanzomon, bristling. "Are you heroes, or are you cheaters?"

Benny and I hoisted the catnip-filled animals high.

The scorp-lions rushed us, frantic for their treat.

I did the only thing I could think of—I thrust the teddy bear into the billionaire's arms and jumped aside. Benny did the same with his pink bunny.

"What the—?" Mr. Hanzomon sputtered.

"All's fair in love and war," I said.

"And science," Benny added.

Alarmed, the billionaire tried to untangle himself from the leashes and dump the stuffed toys. But he was too slow.

Chapter Twenty-Six

A Thin Line Between Love and Bait

PINCERS GRABBED. Paws swung. Monsters lunged. Down went the scientist beneath the weight of his own creations.

"Nooo!" cried Mr. Hanzomon. "Back! Get back!"

It seemed like the scorp-lions were mostly interested in the stuffed toys. But when the scientist struggled to get out from under them, two of the creatures lashed out and stung him—*fwak, fwak!*

He crumpled, moaning, "Oh, the horror."

"Aw, geez," said an Animal Control worker. He made a move toward the downed billionaire. "We should help him."

"Wait a minute," said Benny.

"But he's hurt," said the man's coworker, starting forward.

I held out an arm to stop her. "And you'll be, too, if you don't wait."

"Terrible, terrible," muttered Mr. Hanzomon, staring into space. "All my experiments, a total failure."

I could guess the horrors he must be seeing, having been stung before. Despite myself, I felt a pang of sympathy.

The scorp-lions spun and writhed and bit the stuffed animals. They rolled on their backs like playful mutant kittens, purring like thunder. Finally, they collapsed onto their toys, spent. The monsters' eyes were all pupil, making them look even creepier—if that was possible.

"Okay . . . now!" said Benny.

The Animal Control workers advanced, their elbow-length padded gloves and snare poles at the ready. Blasted out of their minds on catnip, the monsters offered little resistance. Soon the workers had nudged all four of them, along with their stuffed toys, into the cages. When Animal Control locked them up, I finally let out my breath.

Drawn by the commotion, a few kids and parents crowded the doorway behind Esme and Tina, oohing and aahing over the scorp-lions. Several blue-suited Hanzomon employees pushed through the crowd and surrounded their boss. Giving one last whimper—"Undone by . . . schoolboys!"—the billionaire promptly passed out.

Benny and I bumped fists and stood back to watch the hubbub. Within a minute or two, the wail of sirens signaled the paramedics' approach.

Principal Johnson turned up at my elbow. "And that's that?" she said.

"Pretty sure," I said.

She cleared her throat. "We need to talk."

"What about?" said Benny.

"Your putting our wealthy donor into a coma."

I considered reminding her that she was the one who had promised to keep an eye on him, but you can only push things so far with a principal. "Yeah, well, that donor was the person responsible for creating and unleashing those things."

Her eyes widened. "You're kidding me."

"Wish I was."

Mrs. Johnson clucked her tongue. "But he was so generous. And he seemed like such a nice man. . . ."

Benny grunted. "Sure, if you define *nice* as nuttier than a Christmas fruitcake. He's got a whole lab full of monsters."

The principal's eyebrow arched. "And you know this how?"

"Uh . . ." said Benny.

"Don't ask," I said.

She folded her arms. "*Don't ask* meaning you don't know, or *don't ask* meaning I don't want to know?"

"Just . . . don't ask," I said.

After all that hassle, I thought we'd at least win the science fair. But no. Not even an honorable mention. It seems you actually have to be present to demonstrate your project for the judges. And worse, you have to use real scientific methodology. On top of that, nobody even knew what we'd done, as the principal kept the whole thing under wraps.

We settled for a warm thank-you from Mrs. Johnson and the knowledge that we still had one get-out-of-detention-free chit from her.

As the fair was wrapping up, Benny and I stood on the side, chatting with Tina and Esme.

"That's the last time I let you two have all the fun," Tina said. "Next monster that turns up, we're fighting it together."

"Count on it," I said.

Esme wagged her head. "I still can't believe how mean those things were."

"They're *monsters*!" said Benny and I together.

She shrugged. "Even so." Then her face brightened. "Hey, I just had an idea."

"Careful," said Benny. "It can be dangerous your first time out."

Esme ignored him. "Why don't I ask my mom to create some kind of antidote to the scorp-lion poison? You know, something to get those people out of their comas?"

"Um, is your mom a real scientist?" I asked.

Her hackles went up. "Of course," she huffed. "It's hard scientific work, bringing something to life. People think it's all 'Go steal some brains, Ygorre,' but it's not!"

I raised my palms. "No offense."

"I think it's a great idea," said Tina.

Esme grinned. "That's it, then. I'm calling her right now."

"And maybe she and the police can figure out what to do with all those monsters in Hanzomon's lab," said Benny. "Maybe start an Unnatural History Museum?"

"Monsters, plural?" Esme smiled so widely, her ears were in danger of falling off. "That I gotta see!"

"Esme . . ." Tina said, warningly.

They wandered off to do their thing. Benny and I strolled out to the parking lot to wait for Abuelita to pick us up. Now that this danger was past, my mind went directly to the next horror show in my life: the possibility of my parents' divorce.

When the car pulled up, Benny and I slid into the backseat. We greeted my *abuela*, and he elbowed me. "We did it!" he crowed, beaming.

"That we did," I said.

"What did you do?" asked Abuelita.

Benny and I exchanged a glance. "Oh, um, a school project," I said.

"And we covered that 'project' with awesome sauce!" cried Benny.

"And a cherry on top," I agreed, though I felt distracted.

Benny raised his hand. I guess my high five wasn't quite as enthusiastic as he'd expected.

"What is it?" he asked.

"Oh, it's that"—I glanced ahead at Abuelita—"other thing."

His eyes widened in understanding. "Ah." He patted my arm. "Dude, you've got nothing to worry about."

"Yeah, sure," I said, my stomach rolling at the thought.

The car stopped outside Benny's house. The sun had set, and dinner hour was close at hand, but he lingered.

"No, really," said Benny. "After all you've handled? You'll be just fine. You're a real hero." He clapped my shoulder and headed for his front door

I considered his words as we drove off. Could Benny be right? If I'd risen to the occasion in getting rid of the scorpions; maybe I could do the same in other parts of my life. Maybe I could be a sort of everyday hero, even when the monsters weren't around.

Taking a deep breath, I squared my shoulders. Hero or not, it was time to face what was coming.

Chapter Twenty-Seven

Ends with Benefits

A **SURPRISE GREETED ME** in the dining room. Instead of one of Abuelita's delicious meals, a full on Chinese takeout feast covered the table. The rest of my family was just sitting down to it.

After collecting a hug from my mom, I greeted my sister, Veronica, with a "Hey, Ron-Ron."

"Hey, C-Man," she said, with her usual blend of sunny brattiness.

I took in this perfectly normal family scene, and a knot the size of Cleveland formed in my throat. Suddenly it seemed hard to draw a full breath. Was this all coming to an end tonight?

I checked my parents' faces for clues (Abuelita had driven off to play a gig), but they were harder to read

than Scandinavian furniture assembly instructions. For a few minutes, it was all "Pass the spring rolls" and "More moo shu pork?"

My nerves wound tighter. My head throbbed. The suspense was killing me, but I did my best to act normal. I even slipped my dog, Zeppo, a piece of pork.

Then my dad wiped his mouth. "Kids, we wanted to have everyone here together for an announcement—kind of a celebration, actually."

Celebration? I'd heard of putting a positive spin on things, but celebrating divorce? Still, I leaned forward. Half a spring roll lay in my mouth, forgotten.

"It's over," said my mom.

"No!" I cried. Or at least I tried to cry. What happened was, the half-chewed spring roll shot from my mouth and hit my dad smack in the chest.

He looked down at the wet spot. His eyebrows lifted. "We thought you'd be pleased."

"Pleased?!" I half rose from my chair. "That's nuts! Who would be happy about their parents getting divorced? Somebody always moves out, and then you don't get to see them as much as you want, and it's all awkward, and you have to figure out who lives with who, and, and—"

I ground to a halt, mid-rant. My family was gaping at me like I'd just sprouted reindeer antlers and an eagle beak.

"Divorce?" said my mom softly. "Is that what you thought this was about?"

A chuckle escaped my dad's lips.

"It's . . . not?" I asked. I didn't even dare to hope.

"Oh, *chamaco*," said Dad. His big hand rested on my wrist.

"Honey, our marriage is not what's over," said my mom. "But this living arrangement is."

"Huh?" I said. Because I'm good with the insightful questions.

Dad was grinning. "Veronica's show has been canceled. She and your mom are moving back home—full-time."

"Noooo!" screamed my sister. "I *can't* be canceled!"

A whoop exploded from my gut like a beach ball

popping out of a pool. "The show's done? You're really coming home for good?"

"Yes, we are," said Mom.

"That's great!" I yelled.

"It's *not* great!" cried Veronica. "I'm calling my agent!"

I tried to tamp down my enthusiasm enough to give my sister some sympathy. "Uh, I mean, it's great that you're coming back. It totally stinks that your show was canceled."

"Stinks like a big bunch of doody-heads," said Veronica, crossing her arms.

Mom wrapped her in a hug. "So sorry, honey. It has nothing to do with you. They loved you."

I couldn't keep the goofy grin from my face. "Hey, you'll get another acting job. You're really talented."

My sister's pout weakened. "You think so?"

"Absolutely," I said. "That time you stole my ray gun? You had me totally convinced that you didn't."

A small smile broke out. "I *am* a good actress."

My mom and dad laughed.

Boneless with relief, I sprawled in my chair. So life was back to normal again. How about that? I looked around at my family, laughing, chattering, and eating. This, I thought, this is worth fighting for. This is worth trying to be a hero.

And then my phone rang. Fishing it from my pocket, I stepped away from the table. "Hello?"

"Oh, Carlos," said a girl's voice. "You won't believe what's happened."

"Esme?"

"My mom went up to Mr. Hanzomon's place to check on the monsters, and you know what?"

"What?" I asked.

"They're gone. Someone let them out—all of them."

The news should have rocked me. It should have filled me with fear. But instead, I heard myself calmly saying, "Thanks for letting me know. We'll get right on it."

I hung up.

"What was that?" asked my mom.

"Oh, a project for school," I said, sitting back down. "Pass the chow fun?"

Tomorrow, I knew, Benny and I would be back on the job with Esme and Tina. After all, a hero's work is never done.

But for tonight, I'd be with my family. For tonight, it was enough to be home, together, and looking forward to a merry Christmas and hairy New Year.